MW01132332

MOON VALLEY SHIFTERS

VOL 1-3

ARIEL MARIE

Copyright © 2018 by Ariel Marie

Edited by Dana Hook at Rebel Edit & Design

Cover by Studioenp

This is a work of fiction. Names, characters, organizations, businesses, events, and incidents are a figment of the author's imagination and are used fictitiously. Any similarities to real people, businesses, locations, history, and events are a coincidence.

All rights reserved.

No part of this publication may be reproduced, distributed, or transmitted in any form or by any means, including photocopying, recording, or other electronic or mechanical methods, without the prior written permission of the publisher

LYRIC'S MATE

Moon Valley Shifter

Book 1

CHAPTER ONE

Lyric Neminee tried to reel back her wolf, who was anxious to discover their new territory. Wanting to make her own way through life, she had moved to Moon Valley a week ago and her funds were beginning to run low.

It was time for her to report for her new job. She was excited about starting a new chapter in her life. She had left her old pack to make a better life for herself. Being the only child to Harmon and Lilly Neminee, who were looking down at her from Heaven, she wanted to make her parents proud.

She stepped over to her floor-length mirror to take one last look at herself. She wanted to ensure that she looked professional, even though the alpha had told her she could dress casually.

"First impressions are everything," she murmured. It was summer in Moon Valley, and she kept her outfit light to ward off the heat. Her skirt flowed around her knees, and her peasant shirt hung off her shoulders. Her perky breasts were full, and there was no way she would be able to get away with no bra, so she chose a strapless one so that her girls wouldn't get in the way.

At five feet even, she was a small shifter, and heels wouldn't really help her out much, so she chose a pair of flat sandals. She turned and grabbed her bag so she would arrive a little early for her first day.

Being hired by the alpha of her new pack was an honor. She didn't want to let him down and wanted to look her best for her first day on the job.

According to Kortan, the Moon Valley pack alpha, her job was to be the assistant for one of the members of the pack, and would include paid travel. He was very vague on who she'd be working for, but he explained on the phone that she would find out all the information once she arrived.

She hurriedly left her cabin and began the walk to the pack's main house. The inhabitants at the compound were a close-knit community, and according to Kortan, when she was in town, she would be working out of the main house or anywhere she was needed by her employer.

The sun was high in the sky already for it to be

early. She smiled as she soaked in the sun. Her long dark hair flowed around her shoulders as a gentle wind blew. She thought she would be nervous, but she felt more excited than anything. She was ready to jump headfirst into her new career and new pack.

Her wolf picked up the passing scents of animals that were nearby. Her ears perked up, but Lyric quickly reminded her animal that they had to report to work. There would be plenty of time for exploring and hunting later.

It didn't take her long to arrive at the main house. The large stone building was located near the main road. Most of the compound was located away from human civilization, but the main building was located near the strip of shops and cafés.

The humans were aware of shifters, but most times, shifters tended to live near open lands so their animals could roam free. Even the shifters who lived in the city always made their way into the wild to allow their beasts to stretch their legs.

Lyric arrived at the stone building that had Moon Valley Pack embossed on the building front. She stood at the bottom of the stairs and gazed at the building. A sense of acceptance embodied her as she breathed in the fresh morning air.

"Now or never," she murmured. She plastered a smile on her face and scurried up the stairs. Walking

ARIEL MARIE

through the front door, she was met with the coolness of the central air.

"Hi!" An older woman greeted her from behind a reception desk. Laugh lines were etched into the woman's face, which was cradled by soft, salt and pepper curls. One look at the woman and Lyric knew she was human. "You must be Lyric."

"Hello. Yes, I am." Lyric strode over to the desk with her hand outstretched. The woman smiled a large grin as she stood and took Lyric's hand.

"It's so nice to meet you. I'm Pola, the alpha's secretary."

"Thanks. I'm here for a job. Kortan didn't really tell me much about it, though. He just said that it was an assistant job, that it paid well, and included travel. Know anything about it?" Lyric asked, her voice ending on a nervous laugh.

"Oh, my! That's just like the alpha to keep everything to a minimum. Come on. Let me take you to your desk and I'll tell you all about the position." Pola laughed, clasping her hands to her chest.

Lyric relaxed as she followed Pola. She had a feeling that the two of them would get along just fine.

"So, who exactly will I be assisting?" she asked as they came to an office area. There was nothing exciting about it. It was slightly larger than her closet at home, with a large window that sat behind her desk. She turned around and noticed a door to her left.

"You'll be assisting Kortan's sister, Liberty Glenn. She's a famous model," Pola whispered. Her eyes twinkled as she tucked her graying strands behind her ears.

"Wait—Liberty Glenn is Kortan's sister?" Lyric asked, flabbergasted.

Who didn't know of Liberty Glenn? She was only the most famous wolf shifter around. Her perfect face and figure had graced the covers of the most coveted fashion magazines. Lyric swallowed hard. She had a huge crush on the model.

She looked down at her clothes and thought twice about her comfortable clothing.

"Don't worry about how you're dressed. You're beautiful, and Libby's not a snob. Since her career has blown up in the past couple years, she needs someone to help her."

"I'm honored," Lyric gushed. She could feel her lips spread into a wide grin as she thought of her luck. She would be the assistant to one of the most beautiful women in the world. She couldn't wait to meet her.

"Pola!" a musical voice called out.

Lyric's heart raced. She wiped her sweaty hands on her skirt and tried to quickly comb her fingers through her hair to make sure she looked presentable.

"I'm back here with your new assistant!" Pola

called out from the doorway.

Lyric swallowed hard, trying to make sure she didn't act like an idiot when she met Liberty. She was a fucking superstar in the world of shifters. She had blazed a trail in the human fashion world that gave every young female shifter hope at making it in a world that was saturated by humans.

"Anything you need to decorate your office with, or supplies you need to work, just let me know…"

Pola's words were lost to Lyric as her eyes connected with the bright blue ones of Liberty Glenn. She felt her breath catch in her throat as she took in the flawless beauty as she appeared in the doorway. Her curvaceous body was covered by a white spring dress that stopped mid-thigh. Her high, full breasts had Lyric licking her lips, wishing that she could suck them deep into her mouth. Liberty's long golden legs seemed to go on for miles. Her hands itched to part the gold limbs so that she could discover what was in between them.

Her eyes made their way back up Liberty's body, and she felt moisture collect at the apex of her thighs as their eyes met.

Liberty was affected just as much as Lyric was.

Her eyes darted to Pola, who was unaware of the instant attraction between the two women.

"Hey, Libby. Let me introduce you to Lyric Neminee, your new assistant."

CHAPTER TWO

Libby took one look at her new assistant and her wolf slammed against her chest.

She wanted the small female.

Lyric. She loved the name. It was unique and fit her new assistant. She smiled at the woman, knowing that she was attracted to her just as much as she was to her.

Libby could scent the wolf's arousal and held back a growl. She had never had such a strong reaction to anyone before, and definitely not to someone that was supposed to be working for her. She swallowed hard, beating down her wolf who wanted to push forward to get to the smaller wolf.

"I'll leave you two girls to chat so you can figure

everything out," Pola announced as she ambled over to the door. She gave Libby a wide grin and hug.

"Thanks, Pola. You're the best," Libby said, stepping out the way to let her brother's secretary by.

"And don't you forget it," Pola called out as she made her way back to the front.

"Why don't you come into my office," Libby offered. She walked into her new assistant's office and went over to the door that connected their offices. She opened the door for Lyric to pass through.

"I was wondering what was on the other side of this door." Lyric laughed as she brushed past her.

Libby bit back a groan as she took in the pure scent of Lyric. Her natural smell was overpowered by her arousal. It was strong and sweet, and held a bit of tanginess that Libby would love to have on her tongue.

She followed Lyric into her domain and headed over to her desk. She laid her messenger bag on the windowsill behind her chair and motioned for Lyric to have a seat in the chair in front of her desk.

"So, I hear you're new to Moon Valley." Libby figured she'd start out with an icebreaker and find out a little something of her new assistant. Her brother, God love him, always held back most information. According to him, he'd found the perfect assistant, and apparently, that was all she needed to know.

"Yes. I just moved here a week ago. I was ready to

try to find a new job that would challenge me, introduce me to new things, and something I could have fun with," Lyric said.

Libby could sense the nervousness radiating from the little wolf and she smiled, trying to ease her nerves.

"You're not getting interviewed. If my brother hired you then I'm sure you're the best fit." Libby went into further detail of what she was looking for in an assistant. She wasn't looking for someone to do managerial duties, as she already had a manager. She was looking for someone to help her with the daily aspects of her life—her social media outlets, and her business that her manager didn't handle.

She could immediately tell that Lyric would fit right in. She had broken out a notebook from her bag and immediately began taking notes, and even asked questions.

Libby was fully aroused as she watched Lyric. The way the little wolf would hold her pen against her plump lips, her exposed creamy shoulders, had Libby wanting to run her tongue along the exposed skin. Her core clenched with the thought of running her hand along Lyric's curvy body. She was a few inches shorter than Libby, and had soft curves that she wanted to explore.

"Any other questions?" Libby asked.

"Um, yes, Liberty—"

"It's Libby. All my close friends and family call me Libby. We're going to be working really close together, so you might as well call me Libby too," she insisted.

Lyric's eyes flashed at the mention of them working closely together.

"Yes, Libby. I was just wondering about the work schedule. What time should I report?"

"Well, when we're not traveling, I would say about nine in the morning should do."

Lyric stood from her chair and offered a wide grin. Libby's breath caught in her throat as she took in the softened features of Lyric's face.

"I think we'll get along just fine," Lyric announced, offering her hand. Libby stood from her chair, a smile on her lips. She took Lyric's hand and the electrical current that flowed up her arm wiped her smile away. They both jumped from the jolt.

"Yes, we'll be good together," Libby murmured, knowing that her words held a double meaning.

She knew they would be good together. Not in the business sense, but in the sexual sense. She knew she shouldn't pursue her assistant, but she couldn't help it.

She wanted her even more after spending a short time talking with her.

"Go ahead and figure out what you'll need for your office and Pola will look into ordering items for you. We'll just use today as an orientation day."

She walked Lyric over to the door that separated their offices and smiled as she leaned against the doorjamb.

"Thanks for the job, Libby. I won't let you down," Lyric assured her as she walked into her office.

Libby smiled as she shut the door. It had been a while since she'd had a relationship with anyone. Her career had taken off in the past two years, and she hadn't had time for love.

She pushed off the door and headed back to her desk, kicking off her shoes as she sat. Her heart was still pounding away at the thought of her sexy little assistant. A sigh escaped from her lips as she hit the button to turn her computer on. She leaned back in her chair and groaned. The short time she had spent in Lyric's presence had left her sexually frustrated.

Her clit throbbed, begging for attention. A vision of Lyric's curvy bottom sashaying past her as she walked out of her office came to mind.

"What am I going to do?" Libby whispered as she propped her foot up on the edge of her chair. She reached up and pulled her drenched panties to the side to free her aching pussy. The cool air kissed her core, causing a shiver to slide down her spine. Her clit was swollen and puckered, begging for attention.

Imagining her little mate spread out naked on her desk before her, made her pussy clench. Her fingers slid across her swollen clit. She gently began rubbing it as she imagined Lyric's pussy wet and open for her tongue. She bit her lip as a groan built up in her chest. Her fingers flew across her clit as she imagined dipping her tongue deep inside of Lyric's slick pussy. She ached to discover the taste of the little wolf and have her juices coat her face.

She thrust her hips forward, allowing her to angle her fingers to where she could slip two fingers inside of her slick core. She thrust her fingers deep within her pussy, loving the feel of her slick walls gripping her fingers. Her body shook as she silently finger fucked herself.

Her breasts grew heavy as she imagined Lyric freeing them and using her tongue to roll her hardened nipples.

"Yes," she whispered as she increased the pace of her fingers, thrusting deep within her core. Her hips jerked, trying to ride out the waves of the sensations that were coming over her.

Her imagination grew wild as she continued to think of Lyric naked on her desk in front of her. She wanted to bury her face deep within the little wolf's pussy, gather all of her juices on her tongue, and make Lyric fall apart with her tongue stuffed in between her folds.

Libby's fingers were soaked in her own juices as

she added a third finger so she could fuck herself to the brink of orgasm. A gasp escaped her as she reached her climax. She pounded her fingers inside her core as she rode the waves of her orgasm, biting her lip to keep from crying out.

"Lyric," she whispered as she began to come down from her euphoric state. Her fingers finally stalled, remaining buried within her. She slowly pulled her fingers out, only to trail them up to her engorged clit, drawing her moisture up to her sensitive flesh as she drew small circles.

She smiled, knowing that she had the evidence of her release coating her legs. She pulled her fingers from herself and brought them to her lips, wanting to clean her fingers. She groaned as she licked her fingers clean. Soon, she'd be sucking Lyric's juices from her fingers.

CHAPTER THREE

Lyric loved her new position. After a couple of weeks of working with Libby, she knew that she loved the job. Libby was a sought-after model and there were hundreds of phone calls that needed to be screened. She was glad to be able to help Libby with the small things so that she could focus on the important parts of her career.

Libby had gotten her office set up on the first day, and Lyric was able to get right to work. She'd had Libby's social media organized and flowing better. She'd set up some automatic posts of photos of Libby that were taken either by photographers or selfies that she'd asked Libby to send her. She wanted to make sure that Libby's fans felt she was personable and down-to-earth. In the past few days that she'd reorganized

Libby's social media, her likes and follows had skyrocketed.

Aside from the sexual tension between the two of them, their work relationship was perfect. She didn't realize how much it took to be an assistant to a model, and didn't know how Libby had went this long without someone helping her. Next weekend, they'd be flying to the Bahamas for a beach shoot.

Lyric was ecstatic that she got to go with Libby to the islands. She couldn't wait to see her boss in a bikini. She instantly had to suck in the drool that threatened to come forward at the thought of seeing Libby's exposed skin.

Lyric sat on the edge of her chair as she opened the day's mail. Today, Pola was out of the office with Kortan. He'd had an alpha meeting in another territory that was a day's drive away, leaving Lyric to oversee the main building until Pola returned tomorrow. Most of the other offices in the building were closed for one reason or another.

She glanced inside the large manila envelope that was marked fragile, and saw that it held the prints that Libby had been waiting on. She jumped up from her chair and smoothed out her sundress. She had ensured that every day she would come to work dressed in subtle sexiness. She didn't want to be too sexy, but she was definitely feminine, and made sure that her curves were highlighted.

Her heart sped up at the memory of how Libby's eyes darkened as she looked at Lyric's outfit. She knew that her boss had taken notice of her. Every day, Lyric walked around painfully aroused for Libby, and every night, her battery powered vibrator got quite a workout.

She went over to the door that separated their offices and knocked.

"Come in," Libby called out.

Lyric pushed the door open and entered the office. Libby was on the phone, and Lyric paused in the entryway before Libby motioned for her to come in. Lyric held up the manila envelope and Libby pointed to the large table that was situated against the wall.

"How long will we be there?" Libby asked the caller.

Lyric began spreading the photos out on the table, knowing that Libby wanted to inspect them. Each photograph was of Libby in a sexy boudoir setting. Her body was encased in the sexiest lingerie that Lyric had ever seen. Her pussy grew moist just looking at Libby's sexy poses.

What she wouldn't give to be the person behind the camera.

There had to be about thirty photos, and Lyric

made sure she took her time laying the photos out so that Libby would be able to assess them. She was captivated by each and every one of them.

Liberty Glenn was a beautiful woman, and the pictures—as gorgeous as they were—still didn't do her justice.

She leaned her hands on the table as she looked at the beautiful pictures, trying to see if she could pick out the ones that Libby would approve for use.

"They are beautiful, aren't they?" Libby's voice appeared behind Lyric. Her breath caught in her throat.

"They are," she breathed, no longer able to focus on the photos in front of her. Libby's breath gently blew across the back of Lyric's neck, causing her body to tremble where she stood.

Her back was exposed, thanks to the thin spaghetti straps of her summer dress. In this particular dress, the back was low enough that she was unable to wear a bra. She had worn a sweater this morning when she had walked to work to ward off the early morning chill. But since arriving at the office, she had warmed up and took it off.

"This dress has been driving me crazy all day," Libby breathed. Lyric's heart sped up as Libby's gentle fingers ran up her arms as she pressed her breasts to Lyric's back. She groaned as she leaned back into

Libby, loving the feel of her large mounds pressed up against her.

"Really? It's just a plain old summer dress," she whimpered as Libby's fingers danced across her collarbone.

"Oh, no, you knew what you were doing. I haven't been able to take my eyes off you today. All day I've been wondering what you have on underneath here."

Lyric's head rolled back and rested on Libby's shoulder as her fingers danced down her chest and made their way back up to the shoulder straps. She slid the straps down Lyric's shoulders, exposing her naked breasts.

"Every day you come into this office in your sexy little outfits. I've been wanting to tear you out of your clothes," Libby admitted, her lips brushing against Lyric's neck. Lyric smiled, knowing that her ploy had finally worked.

Lyric's breath caught in her throat as a guttural groan escaped Libby's lips.

"Yes," Lyric groaned as Libby's hands came around and cradled her heavy breasts. The cool air kissed her nipples, causing them to bead into tight buds. Libby's soft hands gripped her breasts tight as she massaged the large mounds.

"Such a naughty girl," Libby murmured against Lyric's ear. She rolled Lyric's nipples in between her fingers before tugging on them. Lyric gasped from the slight sting, but it instantly dissipated. "Coming to work with no bra on. You wanted to drive me crazy today, little wolf."

Lyric cried out from the ecstasy of finally having Libby's hands on her. Libby certainly was able to read her. She knew that she had worn the dress on purpose.

"Libby," she whimpered, as Libby continued to play with her heavy breasts. She cradled them, massaged them, and pulled at her beaded nipples. Libby was slowly torturing her, and Lyric loved every moment of it.

"Your breasts are so beautiful," Libby whispered against her ear. She nipped Lyric's lobe with her sharp incisors. Lyric was already fighting her fangs as they threatened to descend. It was a battle of controlling her beast. "What else will I discover underneath this sexy dress?"

Lyric turned her head as Libby's hands began to descend. They ran their way down her stomach and hips. Turning her head to reach for Libby's lips, she covered her mouth as the woman's confident fingers made their way to Lyric's small scrap of panties. Lyric felt a tug on the material and ignored the sound of material ripping filling the air.

She gasped as Libby ripped her panties off of her, freeing her soaked pussy. Libby thrust her tongue into

Lyric's mouth as her finger boldly parted Lyric's slick folds, exposing her aching clit.

A deep moan escaped Lyric as the kiss deepened. It was hot, open, and wet. Libby's steady fingers circled Lyric's swollen clitoris, drawing little patterns on it. She could feel the moisture seep out of her core, coating her boss's fingers as she quickened the pace. Her breaths were coming fast as she felt her release building.

"Feel how wet you are for me," Libby murmured against her lips. Lyric whimpered as Libby's fingers spread her labia, exposing her swollen nub.

"Yes," she hissed before Libby covered her mouth with hers once more. Her legs trembled as Libby's fingers began to rub her clit again. She could feel her release coming for her. Libby slid her fingers down toward Lyric's core, teasing the entrance. She cried out, wanting to feel Libby's fingers deep within her.

She couldn't believe that she was strung so tight, that she would come so quick. Usually by herself, it normally took at least twenty minutes. Five minutes with Libby's fingers buried deep in her pussy and she was ready to blow.

Her wolf began to pace inside of her chest, curious about Libby's animal. She could feel the power of Libby's wolf radiating in the room. As the sister to the alpha, it made sense that Libby's wolf was strong.

It called to Lyric's wolf.

Mate.

Lyric gasped. She tore her mouth from Libby's as she felt her release building.

"Yes! Oh, God!" she cried out, bracing her hands on the table in front of her.

"Oh no. No coming on my fingers. I want to taste your cream on my tongue," Libby growled. She pulled her fingers from Lyric's pussy and pushed her dress down to the floor, leaving Lyric naked.

Her body flushed, Lyric turned to Libby. Libby grabbed her hand and dragged her over to her desk. She followed behind her in a fog. She'd been so close to orgasm that she would follow Libby anywhere just to feel the waves of her release grip her.

Libby pushed items off her desk, sending them crashing to the floor before helping to place Lyric on top. She gripped Lyric's face in her hands and slammed her lips to hers. Her mouth instantly opened to allow Libby's tongue to gain entrance. Lyric wrapped her arms around Libby's neck, securing her to her as she leaned in.

"Lay down and present your tasty pussy for me," Libby ordered, tearing her lips from Lyric's.

Without a second thought, Lyric laid back on the hard-wooden desk and spread her legs as wide as she could, presenting herself to Libby as she was directed.

The growl that filled the air, let her know that Libby was satisfied with what she saw. She could feel her juices running down her thigh as she waited.

"Fucking beautiful," Libby murmured, her eyes locked on Lyric's exposed pussy.

"Please," Lyric begged as she felt Libby trail a finger along her thigh and up to her slick folds. Her core pulsed, waiting for either Libby's tongue or her fingers. She needed a release and at the moment, she wasn't too proud to beg for her release.

"Please what?" Libby asked, sliding a finger deep within Lyric's slick core. She groaned as Libby repeatedly thrust her finger deep inside of her. Her hips automatically thrust forward, inviting more fingers and Libby's tongue. "We're all alone, and I'm going to take my time with this pussy. You've teased me too long to rush this."

She introduced another finger, thrusting them deep.

"Please, make me come," Lyric begged, her body writhing on the desk. Libby was teasing her, building up the anticipating of her release.

"Oh, I plan too, little wolf." Libby gripped Lyric's sensitive breast in her hand as she forcefully thrust her fingers deep. "I've waited for the chance to have this little cunt and I will take it all."

CHAPTER FOUR

Libby's fingers pounded into Lyric's pussy, causing her to cry out. She could feel her release surging inside of her. She was almost there. She began to ride Libby's hand, needing more. She wanted to scream to the high heavens for her to make her come, but she already knew that Libby would make her come when she was good and ready. She closed her eyes tight as Libby's hand gripped her breast, anchoring Lyric to her.

"Look how you've soaked my hand with this delicious pussy juice," Libby demanded. Lyric felt her fingers disappear from her pussy and instantly opened her mouth. Libby stuffed her soaked fingers deep into Lyric's mouth. Lyric sucked and lick her own juices from Libby's fingers. She moaned, loving the taste of herself all over Libby's hand.

Lyric frantically cleaned the juices off Libby's fingers.

"God, this is fucking sexy," Libby muttered, dragging her fingers out of Lyric's mouth. She pushed Lyric's legs apart and lowered her head. The first long swipe of Libby's wide tongue on Lyric's entire pussy had her back arching off the desk.

She cried out Libby's name as her tongue began its exploration. Her tongue stroked her clitoris before lapping up the juices that poured out of Lyric.

"Libby," she chanted as her boss's tongue dove deep within her folds. She reached down and gripped Libby's hair, holding her in place and thrust her hips, riding Libby's tongue. Libby's talented tongue swirled around her clit, teasing her. Her lips enclosed around the engorged bundle of nerves, causing Lyric to shout.

A growl escaped her chest as she sat up on her elbows so that she could see, opening her legs wider to allow Libby to take her fill of her pussy.

Libby latched onto Lyric's swollen clit and hummed as she shook her head. Her eyes locked with Lyric's as she ground her pussy farther into the woman's mouth.

"Please, make me come. Make me come," Lyric cried out. She'd never begged before to climax, and right now, she wanted to be put out of her misery.

A finger slid deep within her core. She could feel

her muscles tighten on Libby's fingers as they thrust deep within her channel. The tension in her body grew until finally, she exploded.

"Libby!" she screamed as her body trembled. She gripped Libby's hair in her hands, holding her in place as she coasted through her release. Tears slid from her closed eyelids as her body relaxed on the desk. The tension in her muscles began to fade.

"Are you okay, my little wolf?" Libby asked as she placed small kisses along Lyric's thighs.

"Mmm..." she responded, unable to formulate a real word. She relished in the soft kisses and caresses of Libby. Lyric smiled as she opened her eyes and gazed into Libby's baby blues. "You are fucking amazing."

Libby laughed as she ran her hands up Lyric's thighs. Her body trembled from the feel of Libby's hands on her.

Mate.

That word popped up again in her mind again. She bit her lip as she stared at Libby, then sat up on the desk and scooted to the edge as she reached for Libby.

"I've wanted you since you first walked into my office, when Pola introduced you," she murmured as she brought Libby into the valley of her thighs.

"Is that so?" Libby asked, placing a chaste kiss against Lyric's lips. She could taste herself on Libby's tongue. Her juices coated Libby's face, showing proof of Lyric's release on her chin and lips.

"Yes," she hissed as her hands ran down Libby's perfect curves. Her fingers gripped the edge of Libby's dress and pulled it up and over her head. The air escaped her chest as she caught sight of the sexy lingerie that Libby had on beneath her dress. "Fuck me."

"I think I already did," Libby chuckled as she unsnapped her bra, freeing her large mounds. The sight of her dark areolas made Lyric hunger for Libby even more.

"Come here," Lyric breathed, gripping Libby by her hip and drawing her closer to her. Her mouth instantly went to Libby's beautiful mounds. She used her hand to bring them up high so she could take the nipple as far into her mouth as she could. She used her teeth to tease Libby as she had teased her.

Libby threw her head back as Lyric continued to tease her. She toyed with her beaded nipples with her tongue before suckling it into her mouth, and moaned as she moved to the other one. She repeated her actions, loving the gasps and groans that rumbled from Libby's throat as she played with her.

"God, I love how you suck on my breasts," Libby cried out, holding Lyric's face in her hands, as if guiding Lyric to her breasts.

Lyric loved breasts, and Libby's were phenomenal.

Perfect.

Sweet.

Hers.

A growl escaped Lyric's chest as her wolf grew possessive of Libby. She gripped Libby's ass and pulled her tight as she continued to suckle her. Libby's perfect ass filled Lyric's hands perfectly as she gripped and pulled on the fleshy parts.

"I want to taste you," Lyric growled, pulling back from Libby's breast. She pushed Libby back and hopped down from the desk.

"Yes. I need to feel your tongue buried deep in my pussy," Libby moaned as she leaned her hands on her desk.

"Don't worry, it will be," Lyric acknowledged as she guided Libby's foot to the edge of the desk. This position gave Lyric direct exposure to all of Libby's assets.

"I've seen all of your famous photos. I'm a big fan of yours," Lyric murmured, running her hand along Libby's plump ass. "Every time I saw you in a tiny bikini, it drove me crazy. I wanted to see your breasts and this pussy of yours."

She stood behind Libby and slid two of her fingers deep within Libby's slick folds. Libby cried out as Lyric set a fast pace. Reaching around, she gripped

Libby's breast as she continued to finger fuck Libby hard.

"Yes. You can see my pussy anytime," she gasped. Lyric was pleased that she held the position.

"That's good to hear." She slid her fingers from Libby's core and trailed her slickness to her clit. She jerked and flicked the swollen flesh, eliciting a cry from Libby.

"Yes!" she cried out as Lyric flickered her engorged flesh. She loved how responsive Libby's body was to her. It was like their bodies were in sync with each other.

Mate.

She trailed her fingers back and dipped them into Libby's channel, grabbing her moisture. She trailed her fingers to Libby's puckered anus.

"Lyric," Libby called out.

"Me thinks someone likes me playing with their ass." She laughed.

"Yes. Slide those fingers of yours inside my ass. Please," Libby begged. She crawled on her desk and braced herself on her hands and knees, presenting her ass to Lyric.

"You're the boss," she murmured, sliding her fingers deep inside the tight channel. She bent forward and ran her tongue from Libby's core, gathering some of the moisture, and bringing it to her puckered entrance for extra lubricant. She added some of her own saliva to the mix as she thrust her fingers deep into Libby's tight ass.

"Yes," Libby hissed as Lyric bent back over and swiped her tongue along Libby's pussy. The taste of Libby exploded on her tongue. She moaned as she thrust her tongue in as far as she could, as she continued to pummel Libby's forbidden hole.

Needing to taste more, she withdrew her fingers and spread Libby's cheeks to take a full swipe of Libby's entire pussy, from clit to anus. She swirled her tongue around the puckered anus, playing with it. She sucked and licked it as the moans and cries increased from Libby. She spread Libby's ass cheeks wide to allow her to have full access to her pink anus, and dragged her tongue back to Libby's slick core. Lyric latched onto her engorged clit, sending her into the Heavens.

Libby's screams echoed throughout the building. Her body trembled as Lyric drank in the juices that flowed from Libby's core, making sure she lapped up every drop. Libby's body fell to the desk, unmoving.

Lyric smiled as she rubbed on Libby's plump ass. She kissed along her fleshy meat, getting her fill of Libby.

"Keep that up and we're going to end up fucking on the floor," Libby chuckled.

Lyric nipped the plump meat in front of her and giggled.

"Is that supposed to be a threat?"

Libby rolled over and sat up on the desk. This time, she pulled Lyric close to her and covered her mouth in a deep kiss. Lyric's heart jumped as the kiss deepened.

She couldn't get enough of Libby.

She wanted more.

"Stay with me tonight," Libby murmured, pulling back from Lyric.

Lyric nipped Libby's bottom lip with her fangs that had finally descended.

"I thought you'd never ask."

CHAPTER FIVE

Libby smiled as she felt herself begin to awaken. After their long lovemaking session in her office, Libby and Lyric had closed up the office and went back to Libby's place. Lyric, at first, had wanted to stop by her cabin to grab some clothes, but Libby informed her that clothes would not be needed once they entered the doors of her home.

She felt a tug at her breast and knew that Lyric was suckling her breast. The way that woman loved sucking her breasts drove Libby crazy. She already feel her pussy grow slick with need.

Libby held back a moan as she listened to Lyric inhale as she took as much of her tit into her mouth as she could. Lyric sucked on her breast hard, drawing it farther. Her tongue rolled Libby's nipple, causing the moisture in between her folds to slip out and run down her leg.

Libby's core pulsed as Lyric took her time, causing a moan to escape her lips. Lyric's head pulled back and their eyes met. A smile graced Lyric's lips as she straddled Libby.

She leaned over Libby and offered her breast to her. Libby could feel her mouth water at the sight of Lyric's beautiful breasts. She opened her mouth and allowed Lyric to place one of her tits into her mouth. She instantly closed her mouth around the nipple, nipping at it with her teeth before soothing it with her tongue.

Libby was so turned on, that her pussy juices ran down her ass crack. She nipped again with her teeth before opening her mouth wide, trying to take as much of the breast as she could. Lyric tried to help her. She could feel Lyric's fingers on the side of her mouth as she tried to push more of her large breast into Libby's mouth.

Lyric pulled back, and disappointment filled her chest as her mouth wanted to continue. That disappointment was short-lived as Lyric presented her other breast to her, and Libby greedily opened her mouth to accept it.

"Suck on them as hard as you want," Lyric gasped, her head thrown back as Libby tried to suck as much of it into her mouth. Her pelvis rocked against Libby's stomach, coating her stomach with her pussy juices. "But hurry, I want to sit on your face."

Libby sucked fiercely on Lyric's breast, seeing that her time would be limited. Libby moved her hand to cup Lyric's soaked pussy, using her thumb to draw circles on her slippery clitoris. Lyric cried out as she thrust against Libby's hand.

She could suck on Lyric's breast all day, yet she wanted Lyric's pussy on her tongue. She rolled Lyric's nipple one more time in between her teeth, causing Lyric to shriek.

"Oh, you're a dirty girl," Lyric chuckled, pulling her breast from Libby's mouth.

"You don't know how dirty I can get." Libby smiled as Lyric shifted on the bed, allowing them both to access each other's pussies.

Lyric pushed Libby's thighs open. She could feel her hot breath blowing across her sensitive flesh. Lyric began to slowly lick her labia, while Libby focused on Lyric's delicious pussy. She arched her head forward and swiped her tongue along her lover's cunt. The taste of Lyric would be forever embedded in her mind. There was no other taste like Lyric. She didn't know what this was between them, but she certainly wanted to see where it went.

Mate.

The word was whispered in the back of her mind.

"Yes," she moaned as Lyric latched onto Libby's clit. A shudder passed through Libby's body as Lyric feasted on her.

Libby began to feast greedily upon Lyric's pussy. She gripped Lyric's ass, separating her cheeks to give her full access to her lover. Her tongue traced every facet of the slick core. She dipped her tongue in, getting her fill of Lyric's juices, her face covered in her lover's arousal. She slid a finger deep inside of Lyric, while she drew slow circles on her clit with her thumb.

Their lovemaking grew frantic as they each wanted to make the other one climax. Libby gripped Lyric's ass and brought more of her pussy to her face so she could feast while Lyric did the same to Libby. They both cried out as they reached their climax together.

Lyric was on cloud nine. She had spent every night with Libby. They had both agreed that they would remain platonic when in the office. She had ran home this morning and showered to try to get Libby's scent off of her. If someone inquired about Libby's scent, she would just say it was from them working in close proximity to each other.

"Morning," she called out to Pola as she entered

the building. It was a few minutes before nine and it was busy. A few other offices in the building were in use.

"Morning, Lyric," Pola called out from behind her desk. She walked to her office, smiling the whole way. She and Libby had been up most of the night making love, and tomorrow, they would leave for Libby's photoshoot in the Bahamas. She wanted to ensure that she had everything ready for Libby. She knew that Libby was going to be late coming into the office today, so it was up to her to ensure that they were ready for travel.

She pulled her keys from her bag and unlocked her office. She entered and tossed her bag onto her desk and booted up her computer before grabbing a bottle of water from her office fridge. With it being the middle of summer, it helped to keep chilled water around. Even with her summer dress on, she could feel the sweat beading at her hairline.

She took a healthy swig of her water as she sat at her desk. She had a lot of desk work she needed to do before she had to do some last-minute running around. She needed to address Libby's emails, her social media, and her mail.

Her computer finally came on and she got to work.

CHAPTER SIX

She hadn't realized how much time had passed until the door between her and Libby's office opened. She jumped and turned, catching the scent of her lover as she breezed through the door.

"Hey, you." Lyric smiled as Libby walked into the room. Her heart sped up at the thought of her lover. She was beginning to think that Libby was her mate, but she wasn't sure how to bring it up to her. Usually, the minute they arrived home after work, their lips would be fused and their bodies would fall into the bed naked, and all conscious thoughts would be out the door.

"Hey, beautiful." Libby winked as she came over to her. Lyric turned as Libby grabbed her head and slammed her lips down on hers, kissing her within an inch of her life. She didn't know what she did to deserve such a kiss, but she wanted to figure it out quick. She would need to do it again. "I missed you, love."

"I missed you too," she murmured as she pulled back. She glanced over at her office door to ensure that her door that led to the hallway was closed. Libby was in a sexy floor-length skirt with a white tank top. It was perfect on her, and gave Lyric easy access to her. "Come here."

She pushed her chair back away from her desk to allow Libby to straddle her lap. Their lips fused again in a deep, passionate kiss.

"I want you with me anywhere I go," Libby murmured, pulling back.

"Really?" Lyric asked, dazed from their passion laced kisses.

"Yes." She laid another quick kiss to Lyric's lips. "I want to be able to reach for you at any time, even if it's just to hold your hand. When we're apart, I miss your smile and how you make me laugh. And if I want to kiss you, I want your lips available immediately."

Just hearing Libby's words, Lyric yanked her head to her so she could crush her lips to her lover's. She felt the same way. She never wanted to stray from Libby's side.

They were meant for each other.

"I feel the same way," she murmured, pulling back. She looked at Libby's heavy breasts and yanked on her tank, not caring if she ripped it open. Her wolf was nearing the surface and wanted Libby.

"Baby," Libby moaned as she threw her head back, thrusting her naked breasts forward. Lyric gathered one in her hand and brought it to her lips. She teased the budded nipple with her tongue before engulfing as much as she could of the orb. She flicked her tongue against the nipple before pulling back to suckle Libby's breast as if she were a babe. "You always know what I need."

"I'm here for you whenever you're in need, my love. Just say the word. I don't give a fuck where we are. I'll fuck you with my tongue or fingers to make you feel better," Lyric groaned against Libby's breasts. She had learned quickly that the life of a model was not as easy as it looked. Libby put in long hours working out and ensuring that her brand was perfect.

Lyric meant it.

Anytime Libby needed her, she would be there for her.

She dragged her tongue to Libby's other breast, sucking as much in as she could. She pulled back and suckled it.

"Make me come, Lyric. I want to fall apart in your arms," Libby whimpered.

Lyric could feel that Libby was strung tight. She ran her hands underneath her lover's skirt and found her naked underneath. They had both stopped wearing underwear beneath their clothing because it was too restricting, and they were ripping them off when they needed each other.

Lyric's fingers dove deep within Libby's folds as she continued to suck, lick, and nip on Libby's tit. She found Libby's engorged clit and knew it would only take a few swipes.

"You're going to have to be quiet," she murmured against Libby's skin. When Libby was in the heat of passion, she tended to be very vocal in their lovemaking.

"I don't give a fuck who knows about us," Libby said, her eyes connecting with Lyric's. Her eyes flashed feral, letting Lyric know that Libby's wolf was nearing the surface. She ground her pelvis against Lyric's hand. "I need you, Lyric. Make me come."

A growl escaped Lyric's chest as her fingers frantically moved on Libby's clit. She sucked Libby's tit hard, determined to make her lover come. If she wanted to scream to the high heavens, then she would gladly make her mate fall apart.

Mate?

Libby cried out as her body grew tense. Lyric

didn't know why, but her wolf kept insisting on what Lyric knew to be true.

Yes, Libby was her mate.

There was no fighting it.

Lyric knew.

Her wolf knew.

Lyric gripped Libby to her as she nipped her nipple before she sucked it back in her mouth. She pinched Libby's swollen nub as she rode her hand. Libby's body shuddered as she let loose a drawn-out scream as she rode the waves of her orgasm.

It was the most beautiful sight that Lyric had ever seen. Her mate's head was thrown back in the throes of passion, with her beautiful, perky breasts thrust forward. Lyric could feel her mate's release coating her hand as she gently continued to draw circles on her slippery flesh.

Libby's eyes met Lyric's as she finally settled down.

Lyric laughed, as she was sure the whole building heard her climax.

"Thank you, my love." Libby smiled as she leaned forward. Their lips fused in a deep kiss. Lyric pulled her fingers from Libby's pussy and offered them to her mate. Unable to resist, she assisted and they both cleaned her fingers together.

"I'm sure every shifter and non-shifter will know

about us now," Lyric murmured, pushing Libby's hair from her face.

"I meant what I said." Libby laid a kiss on Lyric's lips. "I want you with me every day, all day. I want there to be an us, Lyric. I'm falling for you."

Lyric's heart jumped into her throat. Tears clouded her vision as she gazed into Libby's loving eyes.

"I know I'm in love with you," she admitted. Libby leaned her forehead against Lyric's as they smiled at each other. Lyric gathered Libby to her, burying her face in between her lover's breasts. She breathed in her mate's scent and knew that there would never be anyone else for them.

"So, I take it everything is okay in here?" Kortan's voice rumbled from the doorway in between their offices.

They jumped apart, with Libby trying to pull her shirt together to cover herself. Lyric froze in her chair as her eyes went to the alpha's. His eyes narrowed on her for a brief moment before turning to his sister, who still straddled her. Lyric's face heated with embarrassment at getting caught having sex in the office with his sister.

"Yes, we're good, brother." Libby laughed as she leaned forward, gathering Lyric's face to her breasts. Her fingers stroked Lyric's hair, as if trying to assure her that everything would be fine.

"Well, fool around at home. Not in the office." His voice was gruff as he backed out the room and shut the door.

"Oh my God," Lyric moaned.

"What's wrong, baby?"

"The alpha just caught me making you climax in my office," she whined into Libby's skin.

"Oh, believe me, I've caught him in way worse situations. Climaxing on my mate's fingers is the least of his worries."

"Wait—mate? You know that we're mates?" Lyric asked. She knew that her animal felt the call to mate with Libby. If Libby felt it too, then it was nothing but fate that brought them together.

"Yes, my love. I knew it from the moment we met. Now part those sweet legs of yours so I can get a taste of my mate."

"Libby, your brother just caught us," she whispered fiercely as Libby knelt on the floor before her. Even though she was trying to verbally change Libby's mind, she found her legs parting on their own as Libby pushed her skirt out of the way.

Watching her mate fall apart in her arms was a complete turn on. Her own moisture coated her thighs.

"All the more reason he won't return," Libby murmured as she pulled Lyric forward in her chair. She pushed Lyric's legs up, setting one foot on her desk and propping the other one on the armrest of Lyric's chair.

Lyric's pussy was completely open and waiting for Libby's tongue.

"You know you're crazy, right?" Lyric gasped as Libby's tongue dove deep within her folds. Her head fell back against her chair as she basked in the feeling of her mate licking her pussy clean.

"I'm crazy for you," Libby replied. Her eyes locked on Lyric as she slid two fingers deep within Lyric's pussy. She leaned forward and captured Lyric's clitoris in her mouth. Lyric bit her lip to keep from crying out as she rode Libby's magical tongue. Her mate knew how to work her pussy with her tongue and fingers. "This pussy is perfect. Delicious. All mine," she declared, tearing her mouth away from Lyric's pussy.

"Well, if this pussy is yours, then by all means, make me come hard." Lyric cocked her eyebrows, offering Libby a challenge. Kortan catching them was quickly fading as a distant memory as she stared deeply into her lover's eyes.

Her mate sat back with a growl. She pulled Lyric from her chair and laid her out on the floor.

"Challenge accepted."

CHAPTER SEVEN

Libby stretched out on the sandy beach, following the orders of the photographer. The warm sun beat down on her skin. She smiled as she looked into the camera.

"Libby, you're doing perfect," Claude, the photographer, murmured as he snapped photos. He was human, and a highly sought-after photographer. Libby felt honored that the magazine wanted him to shoot her. "Turn your head and gaze out into the water. Look as if you're seeing the ocean for the first time."

She did as directed. She didn't have to use much acting skills as she gazed out into the ocean. She loved everything about being on the beach and she was sure her expression showed it. The crisp blue waters were calm and serene. It was a perfect backdrop for a photo session. When a popular magazine had offered her their cover and insisted it be a beach shoot, Libby couldn't resist.

The shoot may have the readers of the magazine thinking that it was an intimate shot by the photographer, but in reality, there had to be about twenty or more people hanging around. From the production assistants, to makeup and hair, there were a lot of people making her look good for these shots.

After the photo shoot, she'd made plans to take Lyric out in their wolf forms. There were a lot of smaller islands for them to explore. She knew that Lyric's wolf would enjoy running around in the wild parts of the Bahamas.

The shoot ran over much longer than Libby had anticipated. Claude ended up wanting to get morning shots, then some afternoon shots with the sun high in the sky. Her body ached once she was done. She knew that a good soak was coming her way to relieve the stress in her body.

She glanced around the set and didn't see any signs of Lyric. She was the best thing that had happened to Libby. Not only was she a perfect assistant, she was the perfect lover and perfect mate. Knowing Lyric, she was off working, making sure that Libby wouldn't have to worry about anything.

"You were great out there," one of the set crew called out as she walked toward the hotel.

"Thanks." She smiled as she waved to a few of the onlookers. Some of the tourists snapped shots of her as she walked on to the hotel. She could sense their excitement for being witness to a modeling shoot.

She quickly made her way up to their hotel room and yawned.

What a day.

She'd gotten up at four in the morning to ensure she was all dolled up for the shoot. She slid her keycard in the door and pushed it open. She entered the suite and found Lyric working on her laptop at the desk.

"You look dead on your feet, love," Lyric announced, looking up from the computer. Her eyes were wide as she pushed back from the desk.

"That was longer than I expected. I promise, we can go out for a run tonight," Libby promised as she kicked off her flip flops.

"We'll worry about that later. My wolf will be okay," Lyric muttered, pulling Libby into the bathroom. "Let's get you in the tub for a soak."

"You always know what I need," Libby mumbled as she pulled her swim cover over her head. The sounds of water running in the tub calmed her.

Even her wolf yawned.

Yup, she was officially tired. Her body protested as she removed her bathing suit.

"You work so hard. I can't have you falling on your

face," Lyric chuckled as she prepared a bubble bath. Libby walked over to the half-filled tub and tested the water out with a toe. It was warm and heavenly.

"Please tell me you're getting in with me." She eyed Lyric in her long maxi dress that molded to her every curve. She entered the tub and let loose a deep groan as the water wrapped itself around her aching muscles. It instantly began removing all the stresses of the day from her body.

And sand.

One thing about shoots on sandy beaches, sand tended to get into every crevice of her body.

"Nope. You need to relax." Lyric turned the water off and came to sit on the ledge behind Libby, propping a small pillow behind Libby's neck.

"I love you." Libby sighed as her body fully relaxed. She meant it. She didn't know what she would do without Lyric in her life.

"I love you too," Lyric chuckled as she brought her hands to Libby's shoulders and began a light massage.

Libby groaned, turning herself over to the pleasures of her mate's hands on her, kneading the stress from her shoulders. She closed her eyes and laid back and enjoyed the relaxing massage. Her body practically melted as the stress faded from her body.

She could spend a lifetime with this woman, and knew that Lyric was it for her. She didn't want to chance losing the one person she loved and knew what she needed to do. She opened her eyes and reached for Lyric's hand, pausing her. She turned to her, bringing her hand to her lips.

"Mate with me?" she asked. She knew that this wasn't the conventional way to ask someone to create a bond that would be forever. Once wolves officially bonded themselves to their mates, they were a pair that would remain together for all time.

Mating was more than just signing a paper and promising to be with each other for all times as the humans did.

No, a mating was binding your soul to the one person that was meant for you.

Lyric's eyes widened as she stared down at Libby.

"Oh, Libby," Lyric gasped. "Are you sure?"

"I'm sure that it's you who I want to spend every waking moment with. My wolf craves yours and we both know that we're soulmates. We belong together." The water sloshed around her as she fully turned and knelt in front of Lyric.

Lyric's eyes darkened as she took in Libby's wet nakedness. Her nipples tingled from the passion that blazed in Lyric's eyes.

"Libby, I love you so much. I never thought that I would move to Moon Valley and fall in love." Lyric leaned forward and kissed Libby. She opened her mouth and invited Lyric's tongue to duel with hers. She gripped Lyric's head in her hand as the kiss deepened.

"Please, mate with me," she whispered against Lyric's lips. Their eyes met and she saw the love shining in Lyric's eyes. She released a squeal of delight as Lyric nodded her head.

"Yes, I'll mate with you!" She laughed. Libby pulled her into the oversized tub, not caring about the water splashing out onto the floor around them. "Libby!"

She was too excited and her tiredness disappeared. Lyric had just agreed to bind their souls together for all eternity. She was riding on cloud nine.

"I still have my dress on!" Lyric laughed as the water sloshed over the sides of the tub.

"I'll buy you ten more dresses to replace this one," Libby growled, pulling her mate to her. She shifted her hand to allow her claws to come forth as she shredded the dress from Lyric's body. She groaned, finding her mate completely naked underneath the dress. She tossed the offending material to the floor.

Lyric slammed her lips onto Libby's as she strad-dled her body. Their mouths fused together in a hot kiss that was full of tongue and moans. She loved the feel of her mate's slick breasts mashed against hers. She filled her hands with her mate's naked flesh, rubbing

Lyric's body against hers. She squeezed her ass as she pulled Lyric's center to her.

This was her mate.

She tore her lips from Lyric's and latched onto her slippery breasts.

"Libby," Lyric cried out, holding Libby's head close to her body.

Libby wanted her mate to fall apart in her arms. They had much to celebrate tonight. Her hand slid beneath the water's surface and cupped her mate's pussy.

Yes, they had much to plan. She thrust her fingers deep within Lyric and decided they could plan their mating in the morning.

"Tell me again that you'll mate with me," she demanded, needing to hear it. She withdrew her fingers from Lyric's tight channel and slid them to Lyric's sensitive nub.

"I'll mate with you," she whispered, thrusting her hips against Libby's hands.

Ecstatic about Lyric's response, she used her free hand to crush Lyric's mouth to hers. She thrust her tongue deep inside of her mate's mouth, needing to get her taste on her tongue. She tore her lips from Lyric's and trailed her tongue along her jawline and down toward her neck.

Their slick breasts pressed against each other as

she pulled Lyric's body to hers. She didn't want to leave any room in between them. She was aroused by her mate on any given day, but to have her slippery body sliding against hers had her strung tight.

Her hands slid along Lyric's body, having already memorized every facet of her body. She slid her hands down to the plumpness of Lyric's ass and brought her flush against her. Lyric's legs wrapped around her waist, bringing them even closer. The water sloshed around them as they strained against each other.

Their lips fused together as they rubbed their bodies together. Gasps and moans filled the air as they shifted their bodies. They giggled as their legs crossed each other, bringing their pussies flush against each other.

"Libby," Lyric gasped as they rubbed their clits together.

"My mate," Libby growled. She could feel her release building in her as they frantically thrust against each other, the water enhancing the sensation. "Come with me."

Lyric's hand gripped her leg in place as a shudder snaked its way through her body. Their cries filled the air as they reached their peak together.

CHAPTER EIGHT

Lyric's nerves were at an all-time high as she walked to the alpha's home with Libby. Libby squeezed her hand to reassure her. They had just arrived back home from their week in the Bahamas and Libby didn't want to waste any time in requesting that her brother, the alpha, bless their mating and acknowledge them in front of the pack.

"Are you sure he's going to do it?" Lyric whispered, holding onto Libby's arm as they walked up the walkway that led to Kortan's private cabin.

"He's the one that hired you, and technically, that means he hooked us up." Libby laughed.

They walked up the few stairs that led to his porch and Libby turned to her.

ARIEL MARIE

"I know that, but what if he has a problem with us being together?"

Libby's eyes softened as she stared down at her. She stepped close to Lyric and cupped her cheeks with her hands.

"My brother knows how much I love you. This is nothing that will be new to him. We talk about everything," Libby advised. Her lips curved up into small smile as she gently ran her finger along Lyric's cheek.

"Everything?" Lyric chuckled nervously.

"Well, he did catch us in your office. We were bound to have a conversation about him finding me half naked on your lap."

Lyric's breath caught in her throat as the memory surfaced. Their relationship had been a whirlwind, and she wouldn't have it any other way.

"I love you," she breathed, pulling Libby to her. They shared a sweet, gentle kiss. Libby's soft lips moved over Lyric's and made her want her mate even more. She knew that this was the person she was supposed to spend the rest of her life with.

"I love you too," Libby murmured, pulling back. She smiled as she pulled a key from her pocket and inserted it into Kortan's front door. She pushed the door open and waved Lyric in.

Lyric entered the home and found it to be all male,

but cozy. Libby brushed past Lyric and motioned for her to follow.

"Kortan!" Libby called out, walking through the living room and past the kitchen.

"In my office," the alpha's deep baritone voice called out.

Lyric's heart pounded in her chest as she followed behind Libby. They arrived to the double doors and Libby threw her a wink as she pushed the semi-closed door open.

"Hey, big brother," Libby gushed as she ran to her brother. He smiled as his sister threw herself at him. He gathered her in his arms for a hug and a kiss on the top of her head. Lyric knew the siblings to be close.

Kortan was a fierce alpha and protected the pack. She had never belonged to a close-knit pack as the Moon Valley pack.

"Hello, Alpha." Lyric nodded her head out of respect. Her wolf instantly submitted to Kortan's.

"Lyric, how are you?" he asked with his intense eyes locked on hers.

"I'm doing well."

"Please, you girls have a seat." He motioned to the couch. Libby winked at her as she grabbed Lyric's hand, pulling her over to the couch. They sat close to each other while Kortan took the recliner that faced them.

"Brother, we have something that we want to ask you," Libby started, squeezing Lyric's hand.

Lyric's heart raced as she thought of any of the possible responses or reactions that the alpha may have to them requesting to be mated. Female shifters mating with each other wasn't unheard of, it just didn't happen all too often.

"Well, what is it, Libby? I can scent Lyric's nervousness from over here," he chuckled, leaning back in his chair.

Libby glanced at Lyric before turning to her brother.

"We want you to perform the mating ceremony for us. Our wolves have chosen each other," she announced, glancing over at Lyric before turning her eyes back to her brother. "We're in love with each other and want to be together."

Kortan stared at the both of them with unwavering eyes. Lyric squeezed Libby's hand in fear that he would refuse to mate two females. She held her breath as she waited for him to respond.

"Libby," he began, leaning forward in his chair. Lyric's eyes grew wide as her heart raced. "I would be honored to perform the mating ritual for you two."

Libby squealed as she jumped up and down in her seat, while Lyric blew out the breath she was holding.

Libby grabbed her shoulders and crushed her lips to Lyric's in a hard kiss.

"I told you my brother would do it!" She laughed.

"Thank you." Lyric nodded to the alpha. Her heart was filled so much love for her mate that this meant so much to her.

"You make my sister happy and that's all the thanks I need." Kortan smiled as he stood. "When would you like to perform it? The pack will be ecstatic that we're having a mating."

"Tomorrow would be perfect. Is that okay with you?" Lyric asked Libby. Tomorrow was the full moon. The pack did a monthly pack run on the night of full moons.

"That would be perfect." Libby nodded, turning to her brother. "Would you mind? Then we all can celebrate with the run afterwards."

"Tomorrow would be perfect."

Darkness had fallen upon Moon Valley. The sounds of nature greeted them as they walked through the dark woods. Libby's excitement was bubbling in her chest. Her hand tightened on Lyric's as they went deeper into the forest.

Tonight, they would be joined as one.

Her wolf paced beneath her skin, as she knew that soon they would be marking their mate forever. After their marking, they would later join the pack for the official ritual that would be performed by Kortan.

They reached a small clearing that opened up to the sky, showcasing the full moon that overlooked them.

"Oh, Libby, it's beautiful," Lyric gasped as she took in the blanket on the forest floor, and the flowers she had placed around where they would mark each other. She had arrived earlier and wanted to ensure tonight would be special.

"I wanted to make sure you knew how much you mean to me," Libby murmured, pulling Lyric close to her. She smiled down at her mate. Her heart skipped a beat as she looked around, proud of her secret she had hid from Lyric.

"I know you love me, Libby." Lyric closed the gap between their bodies.

Libby smiled as she pressed her lips to Lyric's. Their mouths opened to each other in a deep kiss. She poured all her emotion into it.

A deep need to claim her mate swirled in the pit of her stomach. She knew it was her wolf demanding that they claim Lyric. Her hands slid along Lyric's smooth thighs and settled on the round meat of her mate's ass. A hefty moan rumbled in her chest as she thrust her pelvis against Lyric's. She gripped the offending dress and pulled it up and over Lyric's head, breaking their kiss.

Their eyes locked on each other. Libby trailed a hand down Lyric's cheek and down to the swell of her high breasts. She could hear the quick intake of breath from Lyric as her fingertips trailed along Lyric's beaded nipples.

"I think you're overdressed," Lyric breathed.

"Anything my mate wants, she gets," Libby chuckled. She unbuttoned her shirt and slid it off her shoulders. She quickly disrobed, kicking her skirt off to the side, leaving her naked. Her core pulsed as her mate's eyes trailed along her body.

They knelt on the blanket and reached for each other, falling down on the makeshift bed in a mess of arms and legs. Moans filled the air as their lips moved over each other's. Libby rubbed her aching breasts against Lyric's, drawing a gasp from her. She pushed her mate onto her back and propped herself over Lyric. She smiled as she bent down and placed a small kiss on her lips.

Lyric reached up and took one of Libby's breasts and guided it into her mouth. Libby bit her lip as she watched her breast disappear. Lyric opened her legs for her mate to settle into the valley of her thighs where she belonged.

CHAPTER NINE

Lyric suckled Libby's breast deep into her mouth. She could feel the moisture seep out of her pussy as her mate settled against her open core.

She protested when Libby pulled her breast back, but she was quickly rewarded with Libby's mouth. Her mate thrust her tongue deep into her mouth. She groaned as Libby thoroughly kissed her.

Her hands connected with Libby's breasts, molding them in her hands. Libby tore her mouth from Lyric's and began trailing her tongue along her jawline. Lyric arched her neck to give her mate access to her neck.

Her hands roamed Libby's body as she licked and kissed every part of Lyric's neck and shoulders. Her lips blazed a trail down Lyric's chest. She lavished

Lyric's breasts with her tongue, making sure that each breast was sensitive and aching.

"Libby," she moaned as her mate trailed her kiss farther down her belly. Libby settled in between Lyric's thighs where she was eye level with her core.

"Such beauty," Libby whispered. Lyric's body tensed with anticipation of the sensations of Libby's mouth on her.

She let loose a groan as Libby teased her, running a finger along her slick labia. She widened her legs as she shifted her hips, trying to trick Libby's finger into sliding into her core.

"Don't tease me, mate," Lyric chuckled.

"Oh, I would never do such a thing," Libby drawled, sliding a finger deep into her core. She set a slow rhythm of her fingers thrusting deep inside of Lyric's pussy.

Lyric cried out as Libby covered her pussy with her mouth, her tongue pushing its way into Lyric's folds. She could have wept for joy at the feeling her of her mate's tongue in her pussy. Her hand threaded its way into Libby's hair as she rode Libby's tongue.

Her body shuddered as Libby feasted on her core. Her muscles grew tense, and Libby must have known that she was close to reaching her orgasm.

"No coming yet, my love," Libby murmured, sitting

back up. She spread Lyric's legs wide and leaned forward, brushing her clit against Lyric's.

Lyric cried out as she gave herself to the sensations of their two slippery clits rubbing together. Libby thrust her hips, causing their pussies to glide against each other.

She wanted more.

"Libby," she chanted her mate's name over and over as Libby leaned over her. Libby's breasts swayed with each thrust. Lyric's hands dug into Libby's ass, pulling her as close as they could possibly get.

Her gums began to burn and stretch as her fangs began to descend. Her eyes met Libby's and she could see that her fangs were out as well.

Their breaths came fast as they both were rushing toward release together. Lyric rotated her hips, loving the feel of her mate's slick core against hers. Libby propped Lyric's leg on her shoulder to open her more to her. She leaned down and covered Lyric's mouth with hers, their tongues dueling together as their bodies shifted together in tandem.

Lyric's eyes squeezed shut as she threw her head back, presenting her neck to her mate. A growl tore from Libby's throat as she sunk her teeth into Lyric's shoulder, marking her for all eternity. Lyric gripped Libby to her as she ensured that the mating mark would show. Even with their fast healing capability, a mating mark would always show. It was proof that Lyric belonged to Libby.

She pulled back and brandished her neck for Lyric, who pounced on Libby's shoulder, sinking her teeth into her flesh. The coppery taste of Libby's blood filled her mouth as she took her mate's blood and marked her forever. They both cried out as they reached their orgasm together.

Their cries of ecstasy filled the air as their bodies shuddered. Lyric gripped her mate to her, feeling the lock snap shut on her heart.

Libby was hers. They officially belonged to each other.

"I love you, mate." Libby smiled as she braced herself over Lyric.

"I love you too, mate," Lyric murmured as she shifted her legs and wrapped them around Libby, pulling her close. They were in their own little cocoon of the woods and would be able to celebrate together, making love. It would be hours of loving and marking each other before they would go and meet the pack to have Kortan perform the short ritual that announced their mating.

Their lips met for a deep kiss, knowing that they now belonged to each other in every way that a shifter could.

EPILOGUE

Libby thanked the flight attendant as she ensured that her and Lyric had everything.

"Call if you need anything." Sara smiled as she went to the front of the plane.

"A private plane?" Lyric's eyes were round as she took in the private jet. Excitement was brimming from her eyes.

"Only the best for my mate." She laughed as she grabbed Lyric's hand.

"We could have just flown commercial."

"It's not every day that I get to take my mate on a vacation to a private island." Libby smiled, shaking her head. "Besides, I wanted to have you to myself."

"Well, there is the flight attendant." Lyric gave off a

nervous laugh, pointing toward the direction the woman had disappeared.

"She'll only come if I call for her." She wanted to have Lyric to herself, and she ensured that the crew knew not to disturb them unless she called for them.

They had been officially mated for six months, and Libby wanted to schedule a little getaway with her mate. They had both been working hard, and it was time to relax for a week, just the two of them on a private island. It had been a surprise that she'd kept from Lyric.

She loved spoiling her mate. Lyric meant the world to her and took care of her. It was her way to repay her mate for everything that she did for her.

The plane was finally granted permission to take off. Lyric reached out and gripped her hand as the plane sped down the runway. She knew that Lyric was always nervous, but then again, most shifters were when it came to flying. They just didn't like being enclosed in a flying box. It had taken Libby a while before she got used to flying.

Once the plane was in the air and they had climbed to the altitude the pilot wanted, Lyric finally let go of Libby's hand.

"Here, have a sip of the champagne," Libby murmured as she reached for the two flutes in their cup holders. The luxury plane was perfect for them to relax in as they flew the few hours ride.

Lyric took the flute and downed her champagne in one gulp. Libby chuckled, but knew that her shifter metabolism would run through the alcohol. It would take quite a bit of champagne for them to get drunk.

"You're supposed to sip champagne, not down it like a shot!" Libby laughed.

"I know. My nerves are always high at first when we get in the air." Lyric pushed her hair behind her ear and smiled at Libby, making her heart pound.

No matter how many times they had been together, Libby couldn't get enough of her mate.

"Come here." She motioned for Lyric to come to her. She wanted her little mate and she would have her. She knew just the distraction that would keep Lyric's mind off flying. This was exactly why she wanted to fly privately.

Lyric undid her seatbelt and straddled Libby's legs. Her hands instantly went for Lyric's breasts, cupping them through her low-cut dress. She pulled on the cotton material, causing it to rip down the middle, exposing Lyric's plump breasts. She tore the dress the rest of the way and chuckled as she did the same to Lyric's panties, leaving her mate naked on her lap.

Just what she wanted.

Today, they would be joining the mile high club.

"Libby!" Lyric gasped, a smile gracing her lips.

"I told you I'd buy you ten dresses." She leaned forward and covered Lyric's breast with her mouth. Her mate gasped and threw her head back as Libby sucked. She slid her fingers down along her mate's body and found her naked pussy, waiting and slick.

"You always know what I need," Lyric murmured, her head rolling back down. Their eyes met and Libby smiled against her mate's skin. She pushed her fingers into Lyric's tight cunt and knew that they'd always be able to meet each other's needs.

Right now, Libby needed her mate to fall apart in her arms.

MEADOW'S MATE

Moon Valley Shifters

Book 2

CHAPTER ONE

"Miss Meadow! Miss Meadow!" a tiny voice called out. Meadow Falls turned her head to see one of her kindergarteners running across the playground toward her.

It was a beautiful fall morning, and today, it was her turn to be the recess monitor for the small shifter elementary school in Moon Valley. Children of all ages played together on the large playground. Laughs and screams of joy filled the air. The little girl who was sobbing made Meadow's heart melt. Julie was a little small for her age, but she was a wolf shifter, just like Meadow. She would one day have a growth spurt.

Meadow could relate to the little female pup because she too had always been small for a shifter.

ARIEL MARIE

Standing a little over five feet, barefoot, always gave her a disadvantage to just about everything. Thank goodness for heels! She loved her pumps and the extra three to four inches she gained.

"Yes, Julie?" Meadow asked as the little female wolf slammed into her legs. She ran her hand along the child's head to calm her. "What's wrong, my love?"

"Mitch and Logan are fighting." Tears ran down Julie's cheeks as she leaned back to look up at Meadow. Her wide eyes were full of unshed tears. "And I think Mitch is trying to shift!"

"Oh no! Where are they?" Meadow groaned. Kindergarteners were very unstable shifters. Nature determined that around the age of five and six years old, little shifters could change into their wolf forms. Meadow took off jogging behind Julie as she scurried across the playground.

Tiny, but fierce growls filled the air as Meadow made her way to the small crowd of children that gathered around the two little male wolves.

"Mitch Duncan and Logan Charles, you stop that!" she cried out. Two little wolves were circling each other, eyes locked on each other. She could feel her animal push forward, wanting to break free to discipline the pups who were completely ignoring her.

She couldn't tell which pup was who. From what

the parents had relayed to her at the beginning of the school year, they each had yet to shift. So this meant that the pups would be unstable, needing to learn their places in the pack.

Not wanting to shift, she moved in between the two pups and let her wolf come slightly to the surface.

"Stop!" she growled. Their eyes flickered to hers, but they were intent of settling whatever caused the scuffle. The dark pup jumped at the gray wolf. Meadow grabbed a hold of the pup and lost her balance, falling to the ground. She cried out as her knee met the pavement, and a sharp shooting pain raced through her ankle as she tumbled onto her stomach.

"Boys!" A deep growl filled the air and everyone fell silent. Two large work boots appeared in front of her eyes. Meadow didn't have to look up to see who came to stand in front of her.

The alpha.

She sat back on her bottom with a wince. She glanced up and caught sight of Kortan Glenn glaring at the two pups, who were now whimpering on the ground, eyes cast down. They sensed the alpha before them and quickly understood to submit to Kortan. The other children that had been encouraging the fight took off, leaving the two pups to face the alpha alone.

"Are you all right, Miss Falls?" Kortan asked,

turning his stare to her. Her wolf settled instantly, submitting to her alpha. She nodded her head as he turned back to the boys. "Now, I heard Miss Falls tell you boys to quit and you kept going."

Barks filled the air, as if the boys were trying to explain while still in their wolf forms. Meadow winced again as she took in her bare legs. Today she had worn a skirt and was now paying dearly for it. Both knees were scraped, with blood trickling down her legs. She didn't worry about that, for she knew that being a shifter, she would heal quickly. But it was her ankle that bothered her the most. Her right ankle was swollen and red.

"Shift." The alpha's powerful command caused Meadow's breath to catch in her throat. Kortan's power instantly forced the pups to transform back into their human figures. They both broke out in tears as they sat on the ground.

"Is everything okay over here?" a husky voice asked. A shiver ran down her spine at the voice. She knew without turning that it was one of Kortan's enforcers standing beside him.

Sage Lenzee.

Just the sight of her took Meadow's breath away. She was tall, with her long dark hair free and cascading down her back. Her body was that of an enforcer, toned and slightly muscular. Her cotton shirt and jeans molded to her body.

Meadow had first taken notice of the female wolf when she first moved to Moon Valley six months ago, after graduating with her Masters in Education. Moon Valley school system was one of the best shifter's schools, and it was an honor to be able to grab a position as educator there.

Meadow fought to keep her body from reacting to the female enforcer. Being wolf shifters, anyone within a hundred foot radius would be able to scent Meadow's attraction to the enforcer.

"Sage, take Meadow to the school nurse while I take these boys to the office to get clothed," Kortan commanded. "I'll have the kids go back into their classrooms."

"Sure, no problem." Sage nodded her head as she turned to Meadow.

"Thank you, Alpha," Meadow said. He nodded his head as he grabbed both boys by the arms and led them toward the building. He called out for the children to go inside. Meadow was amazed at how quickly all the children on the playground followed his instructions, but then again, she chuckled, he was the alpha.

Meadow held back a curse as she tried to get the shoe off the foot that was now swollen to three times its normal size.

"That doesn't look good," Sage murmured as she knelt down beside her. The damn thing wouldn't budge. "Here, let me help."

Meadow watched with bated breath as Sage moved to her foot and gently took hold of the offending heel. She bit her lip as Sage wiggled the shoe.

"I'm Meadow," she gasped as the shoe finally came off. She wiggled her toes to ensure that they worked. Sage's green eyes glanced up at her, a small smile on the edges of her lips.

"I know," she said, sitting back on her haunches. Her eyes took in the black and blue mess of Meadow's ankle. "It's my job to know members of the pack. Especially the new ones."

"Oh." Meadow swallowed as she tried to move her ankle, but Sage put a hand on it.

"I'm Sage, by the way." Kortan's enforcer smiled at her, with a twinkle in her eyes.

"I know who you are." Meadow rolled her eyes as a smile played on her lips. Their eyes locked, and Meadow could see Sage's eyes deepen as they continued to stare at each other. Meadow couldn't fight her body any longer. She could feel herself growing moist as Sage finally broke the stare and her eyes traveled down, taking in her body.

Her breasts pushed against her top, feeling heavy as Sage's eyes paused on them. Since she was getting assessed, she took her time in studying Sage. She could see the impression of the enforcer's nipples pushing against her top. Meadow licked her lips as the thought of taking Sage's breasts deep into her mouth appeared. She could feel her arousal soaking her panties and knew that the enforcer would be able to scent it.

She didn't care.

A low growl filled the air. Her eyes flickered up and she caught sight of Sage staring at her again. Her breaths came quick as she returned the stare, knowing that Sage had scented her.

"I better get you in to see the nurse," Sage murmured, blinking her eyes. She snatched the other shoe off Meadow's foot before moving.

Meadow nodded her head as Sage brought her up in a standing position and allowed her to lean against her. She gasped as she felt the womanly curves of the enforcer. Her breasts pushed painfully at her blouse, demanding to be let free.

Meadow leaned into her, trying to stay off her ankle. The pain was too much to bear. Meadow cried out as she hopped on one foot. Sage grabbed her and lifted her up in the air, bringing her body against her chest.

As shifters, they were all naturally stronger than their human counterparts. Their eyes met, and

Meadow swallowed hard, unable to fight the attraction, and by the looks of Sage, she wasn't even trying.

"Thanks," Meadow murmured, wrapping her arms around Sage's neck as she began walking toward the school. She breathed in the scent of Sage and knew that it was one that she would never forget.

CHAPTER TWO

Sage's wolf pushed as it ran through the woods. She was on patrol tonight, and her shift would be ending at midnight. She had the next few days off and was going to use those days to kick back and relax.

As she slowed to a trot, her thoughts turned to a certain new kindergarten teacher.

Meadow Falls.

It had been a few days since the incident at the school where she was able to finally put her hands on the female. Sage could feel the lips of her wolf turn up in a grin. The little teacher was an attractive woman and held Sage's attention from the first moment she saw her. Sage had wanted to connect with her immediately, but she figured she'd give the small wolf time to get acclimated to Moon Valley.

Just the feel of the woman in her arms had her wolf pacing back and forth, just beneath the surface. She had to push her animal down when she realized that Meadow was injured. The small teacher should have known better than to get in between two newly shifting wolves. She could have been hurt worse then scraped knees and a twisted ankle.

New pups were unpredictable. They could have bitten the school teacher or scratched her with their newfound claws.

Her wolf slowed, and Sage looked around. She chuckled, finding her wolf had led her to the small cabin of Meadow Falls. She rolled her eyes at her animal. Of course it would lead her there. If caught prowling the school teacher's yard, she would just use the excuse of patrolling the pack's land.

She kept to the edge of the woods and saw a soft glow on the porch. She moved to the edge and peered out from behind a tree, and with her shifter vision, could see Meadow on her back porch, reading by a lamp. Her foot was propped up on a foot stool.

Why was she up at this time of night?

Sage's wolf whimpered softly, wanting to go to her. She watched as Meadow paused and looked up.

Sage cursed.

With her shifter hearing, she probably heard Sage's animal. She watched as Meadow stood from her chair and walked to the edge of the porch. There was a slight limp, but only someone looking for it would notice it. The small woman was wrapped into a thin robe. She tightened the ties around her waist as she paused.

"Hello?" Meadow called out, leaning against the banister on the porch. "Anyone there?"

Sage found her animal making her way toward the porch. Meadow cocked her head to the side as she warily watched as Sage made her way to her. She stopped at the bottom of the stairs. Her wolf grinned a wolfy smile to Meadow, who chuckled.

"Let me see. Who would possibly be patrolling my lands at this time of night?" Meadow slowly made her way down the stairs and sat on the stair before Sage's wolf. She reached out a hand and ran her fingers along the top of Sage's head. Her wolf whined, pushing her head against Meadow's hand. She laughed as she scratched behind Sage's ears. "You're a beauty."

Her wolf was totally enjoying the attention. Meadow giggled as she ran her hand along the length of Sage's wolf's head.

"Okay, beautiful. It's nice to officially meet you, but can I talk to Sage?"

Sage's wolf released a snort. Her wolf always tried to act like she was in control, but they both knew that Sage was the stronger of the two. She'd had enough time out today, so Sage pulled back on her animal, allowing the change to happen. Her body went through the brief transition, leaving her kneeling before Meadow, completely naked.

Sage's heart pounded in her chest as she stared into Meadow's dark eyes.

"Hi," she murmured, uncaring that she was out in the open, naked. Nudity was second nature to shifters. It was late at night, and they were in Meadow's back yard that faced the woods. No one would see her.

"Hi yourself," Meadow murmured. Her eyes trailed down Sage's naked form. Her nipples beaded into painfully tight buds, and her breasts grew heavy, wanting Meadow to touch them. Her core pulsed with the thoughts of the woman's fingers sliding between her swollen labia. She could feel the moisture collecting at the apex of her thighs. "What brings you here?"

"You," Sage admitted. Meadow's eyes widened at the honesty of the answer. "I was thinking of you and wondering if you'd healed, and before I knew it, my wolf brought me here."

"I guess I should thank your wolf," Meadow chuckled slightly. The sound of her laughter made Sage's heart slam against her chest.

"Why?"

"Because I was thinking of you too," she admitted shyly.

Sage's wolf howled on the inside, pleased that Meadow was thinking of her. She crawled up onto the bottom stair, causing Meadow to lean back on the stairs and part her legs where she sat. Sage's eyes took in the thin robe that covered Meadow's body, and could scent her arousal. It was a delicious scent that made her remember the day on the playground where she'd smelled it before. She licked her lips as she reached for the ties that rested on Meadow's abdomen.

"What were you thinking about?" she murmured as she pulled on the cotton belt, unknotting it. The robe fell apart, revealing a very naked Meadow in front of her. She groaned as she took in the soft curves.

Her body was perfect, and all woman.

Her full breasts called to Sage. Her nipples beaded up into hard beads as the air caressed them. Sage's eyes trailed down to her soft stomach that was tapered in, but flourished out with her wide hips. Her eyes dipped down to Meadow's valley, finding it bare.

"You looking at me the way you are now..." Meadow whispered. A soft wind blew, kissing her skin. A chill slid down her spine as she memorized every part of Meadow's curvy body.

Sage leaned forward, unable to resist taking one of her nipples into her mouth. Grabbing Meadow's plump breast, loving how it spilled out over her hand, she met Meadow's gaze as she sucked the soft flesh deeper into her mouth.

Her tongue rolled the hard nipple around before she nipped it with her teeth, fighting to keep her incisors from descending. Her gums burned, but she was able to control it.

She released the mound and trailed her tongue along Meadow's skin, tasting her. Her wolf howled again, loving that they were finally getting a taste of the little wolf they'd had their eyes on since she arrived in Moon Valley.

She trailed her tongue up Meadow's neck, nipping the skin along the way, loving the feel of Meadow's hands as they gripped her ass, pulling her in between her spread legs. The scent of her wet pussy drifted up to Sage. She nipped Meadow again, before trailing her tongue up her chin and finally to her destination.

Meadow's plump lips.

She crushed her mouth to Meadow's, who immediately opened and invited her tongue inside. Sage braced her hands on the stairs as Meadow wrapped her legs around her waist. The kiss deepened as she angled her head, needing to learn the taste of the woman beneath her.

Their breasts rubbed together, causing Sage to gasp as her sensitive nipples dragged against Meadow's. She broke the kiss and trailed kisses along Meadow's neck and farther down her body.

"The scent of your pussy is driving me crazy," she murmured as she rolled Meadow's nipple with her tongue. "I bet your pussy is drenched for me."

"Yes," Meadow hissed, throwing her head back as Sage trailed her tongue down her abdomen. "Please, have a taste."

She swirled her tongue around Meadow's navel as she knelt on the bottom stair. She pushed Meadow's soft thighs apart so she could study her glistening pussy in the darkness. The soft glow of light from Meadow's lamp on the porch gave her enough light to see the awaiting pussy.

It was absolutely gorgeous.

Meadow's two little plump pussy lips were swollen with need, hiding her clit.

"Look at all that honey making its way out of you," she murmured as she traced the slick labia with her fingers, causing Meadow to moan. "You're absolutely breathtaking. Spread eagle on these stairs. I wish I had a camera to keep this image forever."

"Please," Meadow begged, her head falling down to where their eyes could meet.

"Please what?" Sage whispered, sliding a finger into Meadow's core. Her finger was enveloped into Meadow's slick, hot center. Her tight pussy clenched down on Sage's finger. "Do you know how long I've waited to approach you?"

"No," Meadow whimpered as she rotated her hips against Sage's hand.

Sage added another finger, loving how slick she was. The moisture from Meadow's hot cunt drenched her hand. Her tongue tingled in anticipating of tasting the delectable pussy. She wanted to bury it deep within Meadow's folds and lap up all the moisture that was seeping out onto her fingers.

"Since the first day you walked around our pack meeting, introducing yourself to the families. I can still remember that little dress you wore and those fucking heels you love wearing."

She used her free hand to push Meadow's legs wider and leaned forward to part her plump labia with her tongue. The taste of Meadow exploded on her tongue as it dove in and found Meadow's buried clit. She groaned as she gathered Meadow's juices on her tongue.

"Sage!" Meadow called out as she encircled the little bundle of flesh with her tongue. She caught it in between her lips and pulled back slightly, causing Meadow to cry out. She pulled her fingers from her channel and spread open her labia. She covered Meadow's entire pussy and swallowed Meadow's juices as she continued to feast on her perfect pussy.

She closed her eyes as she continued to devour her lover.

Her woman.

Her wolf growled as she paced beneath the surface.

Sage groaned as Meadow's small fingers threaded their way into her hair. Meadow growled as she rode Sage's face.

"Oh, God! Please don't stop!" Meadow cried out as Sage began to hum her pleasure. She locked onto Meadow's clit, sucking it as far as she could in her mouth, using her tongue to soothe the sensitive flesh. She focused on the little bundle of nerves, wanting to watch Meadow fall apart. She pulled on it again and flickered the little nub with her tongue unmercifully.

She wanted Meadow to scream her release.

She inserted her fingers back into Meadow, thrusting them hard and deep as she sucked her clit. Meadow's body trembled, letting Sage know that she was on the edge.

Just what she wanted.

She twisted her fingers and found the spot she was looking for.

Meadow's muscles tightened. Her legs clamped down on Sage's head as she let loose a scream as her orgasm slammed into her.

"Sage!"

Sage smiled as Meadow's body collapsed on the stairs. She lapped up her lover's release, pleased that it was her name that was screamed to the high heavens.

But she wasn't even close to being done with Meadow yet.

CHAPTER THREE

Meadow sighed as she opened her eyes, then smiled as the memories of her night came to mind. After their lovemaking on the stairs, they went into Meadow's home and continued throughout the night.

She glanced over at the window as she layed on her stomach, smiling wider as she felt a presence hover over her back.

Sage.

"Morning, sunshine," Sage murmured as she placed a kiss on Meadow's shoulder blade.

"Good morning," she chuckled as Sage trailed a line of kisses along her back.

"How did you sleep?" Sage asked, her lips moving along Meadow's skin, stopping at the small of her back.

"What little sleep a certain enforcer let me get? It

was good," she moaned as she felt Sage part her ass cheeks.

"Well, that person sounds cruel," Sage noted as she trailed her tongue along the crack of Meadow's ass. Meadow arched her lower back and propped her knees up to open herself more for her lover's devious tongue.

Meadow could feel herself growing slick with need again as Sage's tongue swirled around her puckered anus. Her face pushed down into her pillow as she turned her body over to her talented lover. Sage ensured that no part of Meadow's body was forgotten throughout the night.

In her new position on her knees, her heavy breasts hung, brushing against the cotton sheets, teasing her sensitive nipples. She spread her legs wide as Sage focused her attention on Meadow's forbidden entrance.

"I can't find one part of your body that I don't like," Sage said, parting Meadow's labia with her fingers.

"Maybe you need to keep exploring." After the multiple orgasms Sage had given her, the enforcer could do whatever she wanted with Meadow's body. She thrust her ass to Sage's mouth as she continued to lick and play with her dark hole.

"Is that right?" Sage chuckled, nipping Meadow's ass cheek with her sharp incisors. Meadow jumped and giggled before her body tensed, feeling Sage's finger rub on her back entrance. "Relax, baby. I'm going to make you feel real good."

Sage dipped her fingers into Meadow's slick core, gathering her juices, and trailed it up to her back entrance. She could hear Sage add her saliva as she pushed one finger into Meadow's dark channel.

She released a groan as the finger of her lover gently stretched her out. The sensation made her pussy clench with need.

"Sage. Please, more," she cried out as she felt Sage nip her ass cheek again.

"Certainly. Anything for you, lover." Sage's husky chuckle filled the air as she pulled her finger back, and this time, introduced a second finger inside of her. Meadow cried out, pushing her ass to Sage, loving the feeling of being stretched and filled in this capacity. Sage began to thrust her fingers, fucking Meadow's ass in a steady rhythm.

Meadow loved it. She rocked back, meeting her lover's fingers as they pounded into her forbidden channel.

Meadow reached underneath herself and found her own pussy with her fingers. Her fingers dove into her folds, gathering her moisture and dragging it to her swollen clit. Her breaths were coming fast as she began to frantically massage her sensitive nub.

"Let me take care of you," Sage growled, pushing Meadow's hand from her pussy.

Meadow cried out as she braced herself on the bed as Sage expertly took care of her with both of her hands. Her fingers stayed buried deep in Meadow's ass while she used her other hand to flick Meadow's clit.

"Yes," Meadow chanted repeatedly, unable to form any other words as she became overwhelmed with the sensations that Sage was bringing out of her. She cried out as her body shook through her orgasm. Her scream echoed through the room as her arms gave out. Her head crashed onto her pillow, leaving her ass in the air.

Her body shook with the aftershocks of her orgasm. She felt Sage's fingers withdraw from her ass, and was replaced with her lips and tongue as she cleaned her. Sage didn't waste any of Meadow's release, licking her entire pussy clean.

"Are you okay?" Sage asked, coming to lay next to Meadow. She pulled Meadow's body to hers, cradling her to her chest. Meadow rested her head against her lover's breast as she fought to catch her breath.

"I am now," she chuckled as Sage tightened her hold on her. She basked in the feel of her lover holding her. She tried to steady her breathing to calm herself down from her explosive release.

Wrapping her arm around Sage, loving the feel of their bodies meshed together on the bed, she was hoping that they would be able to spend the entire day together. Since she was injured on the job, they had urged her to take a few days off, even though she had healed completely. She wouldn't have to report back to work until Monday.

"I'm glad that I could help you," Sage murmured, running her fingers through her hair. "I truly didn't know my wolf was bringing me to your house, but I'm glad she did. Apparently, she was tired of me waiting to approach you."

Meadow chuckled as she trailed her fingers down Sage's lower back. Her wolf was extremely pleased at the moment, laying content inside of Meadow. She knew that if she were to shift, her wolf would have her silly grin that wolf's had when they tried to smile in their animal form.

She just wanted to stay as they were, in their little cocoon of lovemaking. She didn't know what was going to come of this. Were they going to officially date each other? Was this just a one-time thing so Sage could scratch an itch? Was this going to blossom into something more? She didn't know, and didn't want to ruin the mood by asking questions. She didn't know if she would like the answer if it wasn't what she wanted to hear.

But what did *she* want?

Did she want a relationship with this woman?

Yes, a voice whispered in the back of her mind.

Right now, she didn't want to address the elephant in the room.

Nope, she would lay here in the arms of her lover and see where the day took them.

She rubbed her face along Sage's soft skin and smiled. She was happy for the moment. Since moving to Moon Valley, she had made friends, started a job she loved, fell in love with her pack, and now she had the woman of her dreams in bed with her.

She was going to make the most of today.

And right now, a perky nipple gained her attention. She shifted her head and covered the nub with her mouth. She could hear the laughter rumble in Sage's chest as she suckled at her breast.

"And here I thought I'd worn you out," Sage murmured as she ran her fingers through Meadow's tresses. Meadow smiled as she used her hand to steady the plump mound, bathing the beaded nipple with her tongue. She licked the entire surface area of the mound before suckling as much of the Sage's soft flesh inside of her mouth.

Her eyes shifted up and met the loving gaze of Sage as she continued suckling her breast. Sage's gentle fingers ran down the side of her temple and to her cheeks, before going back up to her hair. She shivered as her lover's fingers danced along the base of her neck, cradling Meadow's head to her breast as she shifted more on her back.

Meadow's free hand went to Sage's other breast, caressing it. She pulled on the taut nipple before releasing the other from her lip. She guided the other one into her mouth so that she could pay the same attention to it as she did its mate.

"You've given me such pleasure, I just want to return the favor," she murmured, releasing the sweet flesh. She licked it again, playing with the beaded nipple as she glanced up at Sage.

"Well, with a body like yours, the pleasure was all mine," Sage gasped as Meadow flicked her nipple again with her tongue.

She could feel herself growing aroused again. She had never been turned on like this before. She could feel her moisture run down her leg as she took her time teasing Sage. Usually with her past lovers, a few hours would do her good, but with Sage, she wanted this woman with a passion she didn't know existed.

It was like she needed to consume her.

Take all of her.

"Mate her," a voice whispered.

She felt her eyes widen at her wolf's whispered words as she pushed Sage fully onto her back. Females mating was rare. When she first moved to Moon Valley, she was shocked to find that the alpha's sister had mated her female mate. She'd met Libby and Lyric, and anyone could see that the two were meant for each other.

Was Sage her mate?

She parted Sage's thighs and settled in between them, bringing herself eye level with her lover's glistening pussy lips. She smiled and licked her lips. Sage's mound was void of any hair, and her labia was swollen, ready for Meadow.

The bed dipped as Sage propped herself on her elbows so that she could watch. Their eyes connected as Meadow covered Sage's entire pussy with her mouth, pushing her tongue deep within the moist folds of her lover. Sage cried out but didn't break their gaze.

Maybe her wolf was on to something.

CHAPTER FOUR

Sage strolled into the small elementary school just as the bell sounded off, noting the end of the day. Classroom doors flew open with children rushing to get out. Sage chuckled, remembering that feeling of excitement at the end of the day when she was a child. She could remember running as fast as she could out the door so she could get home. She dodged the steady flow of children scurrying to leave school.

Moon Valley Elementary School was similar to the elementary school she had attended growing up. It was for shifters and ran by shifters. But Sage couldn't remember ever having a teacher as hot as Meadow Falls. She strolled through the hallway toward Meadow's classroom.

Today was her last day off before she had to report

back for duty, and she couldn't wait any longer to see Meadow. They had spent the entire weekend together, never leaving Meadow's small cabin in the woods. They had made love countless times, cooked together, and learned all about each other.

Sage couldn't say that she'd ever felt any closer to another person before. She'd never grown close to her past lovers because she knew they weren't her mates. She was holding out for the one that she would spend all eternity with, so she never allowed herself to get attached.

But something was different about Meadow.

Sage's wolf was content with her, loved the attention she had shown her, and would not leave Sage alone today. Her wolf wanted her to go to the school this morning, but Sage knew that she couldn't interrupt her lover while she was educating her beloved kindergarteners.

Sage smiled as the last of the students made their way through the hallway. Mrs. Thorson made her way from her classroom, closing the door behind her.

"Hi, Sage. What brings you here?" the older woman asked, pulling her messenger bag over her shoulder.

"Just visiting Meadow." Sage smiled, stopping in front of Mrs. Thorson.

"Oh, Meadow. Yes, it was crazy last week with the

two students shifting and knocking her down. She seemed to be doing okay. That was nice of you to help out."

"I'm glad the alpha and I just happened to be here. You know how newly shifting pups can be," Sage chuckled.

"That I do. Meadow's just a sweetie. She's new to town, ya know. Why don't you introduce her to some of the enforcers? I've seen a few of them eyeing her around town." Mrs. Thorson patted her on her arm as she moved past her. "I've got to go. Tell your mother I said hello."

Sage stood in place, biting her tongue. She had always been raised to respect her elders. Her eyes narrowed on Mrs. Thorson as she walked down the hallway.

Introduce Meadow to the guys? They'd been eyeing her?

"Hey." A soft voice broke through her thoughts. She turned to find Meadow leaning against the door-jamb of her classroom. They were alone in the hallway as the last kid made his way down the hallway. "What's got you so upset?"

Meadow looked radiant in her skirt that flowed around her knees, and a low-cut shirt that displayed the tops of her beautiful mounds, but was made appropriate with a light sweater. Her hair was pulled up in a high ponytail, but still flowed down her back. Sage's eyes trailed down Meadow and found her once again in sexy high heels.

Meadow was the epitome of a sexy school teacher. She only needed the nerdy glasses to complete the look.

All thoughts of Mrs. Thorson's remark flew out the window. She blew out a deep breath as she took in Meadow's smile.

"Nothing at all. I was coming to see you," she murmured, walking toward her. Meadow's eyes deepened as she picked up on Sage's vibe. She wanted her sexy teacher.

"*Mate*," her wolf whispered.

"Come on in and let me finish cleaning up." Meadow waved her into her classroom. Sage walked in and instantly felt like a giant. She chuckled at the small desks and chairs that were scattered around the room. "Give me five minutes. I let the kids slide on cleaning a few things today."

"Take your time. I just couldn't wait to see you," Sage admitted, leaning against Meadow's desk, not wanting to risk sitting on one of the small chairs.

She watched Meadow scurry around the room, putting books back on bookshelves and tossing a few toys in a toy box in the corner of the room. Sage's eyes moved to the windows. Meadow's classroom faced the woods. She was sure it was a great opportunity to teach the kids about nature. She could imagine Meadow pointing out wildlife as they strolled out of the woods.

"Won't be much longer," Meadow called out from a small room that was connected to the classroom.

Sage pushed off from the desk. Glancing over at the door, she saw that it was closed. She made her way to the back of the room and found Meadow in a large storage room, putting away a few items the kids must have left out. She watched her stretch up to place a stuffed animal on a high shelf.

"Did I tell you how much I missed you?" Sage asked, walking up behind Meadow. She wrapped her arms around her, pulling her curvy body back against hers. She pressed her aching breasts against Meadow's back and breathed in her scent, knowing that she would never tire of smelling it.

"I don't remember," Meadow giggled. Sage couldn't help dipping her head down and trailing her tongue along the curve of Meadow's neck. "Maybe you should tell me now."

"I missed you so much. I even put on clothes to come see you here," Sage murmured against Meadow's neck. Her hands made their way around to Meadow's breasts, and cupped the heavy mounds in her hands.

"You look cute in your shorts and tank top," Meadow whispered as Sage squeezed her breasts.

"Thank you, my little sexy school teacher." Sage nipped at the juncture where Meadow's shoulder and neck met. She reached up and tucked her fingers underneath Meadow's top and pulled it down, exposing her breasts. "I surely don't remember my teachers wearing outfits and heels like this."

"You poor thing," Meadow groaned as Sage undid the clasp of her bra, freeing her bountiful mounds. Sage gripped her lover's breasts in her hands as the thought of Mrs. Thorson's comment came to mind.

Introduce Meadow to the other enforcers?

Meadow's soft moan filled the air as Sage pinched her hard nipples.

Fuck no.

This woman was hers.

She released a growl as her right hand slid down and disappeared beneath Meadow's skirt. She gripped Meadow's small scrap of panties and pulled them with her wolf strength, tearing the material from her body.

"This is mine," Sage growled against Meadow's neck. Her fingers dove in between Meadow's labia, finding her pussy drenched. She circled the swollen nub of flesh that begged for attention.

"Sage," Meadow gasped as she ground her pussy against Sage's hand.

"Tell me that this pussy is mine," Sage demanded.

There was no way that she'd be introducing Meadow to any male without her mark on her.

Meadow belonged to her.

Sage continued to fondle Meadow's breast as she flicked her finger over the swollen little nub.

"Yes," Meadow hissed, grabbing hold of the shelves in front of her. She propped her leg on the shelving unit, giving Sage better access to her pussy.

"Smart girl." Sage thrust two fingers deep into Meadow's slick channel. She brought Meadow back against her so that she could continue to finger fuck her and reach around her with her other fingers, and began to strum her clit.

"Sage." Meadow chanted her name over and over. She turned her head, allowing Sage to cover her mouth with hers as she whimpered.

Sage knew that her woman was close to falling apart. She knew that they shouldn't be fooling around in Meadow's storage room in her classroom, but she needed her, and right now she had her.

Her hands were completely filled with Meadow's pussy.

She thrust her tongue into Meadow's mouth, sensing that Meadow was close to releasing, but Sage wanted it in her mouth. She broke the kiss against Meadow's protest and pulled her fingers from her lover's pussy.

"Why did you stop?" Meadow gasped as Sage turned her around.

"Oh, I'm not done with you. I want your pussy on my tongue when you climax. Brace yourself," she ordered, kneeling in front of Meadow. She snatched Meadow's skirt off, leaving her barely dressed. Her exposed breasts, shirt bunched around her stomach and her sweater covering her arms, had to be one of the sexist sights that Sage had ever seen.

Meadow held onto the shelving unit. Sage propped Meadow's leg on her shoulder, opening her pussy to her lips. She covered Meadow's pussy with her mouth, eliciting a moan from Meadow as her tongue slid between her slit. She lapped up the juices that ran from Meadow's core.

Her tongue was on a mission to make Meadow fall apart. She slid her fingers back inside of Meadow's core as she latched onto her swollen clitoris. She suckled the bundle of flesh deep into her mouth as she finger fucked Meadow.

"Yes! God, yes!" Meadow cried out, uncaring that they were still in her classroom.

Her juice flowed, coating Sage's face as she feasted on her woman. She thrust her fingers deep as she pulled onto Meadow's clit, feeling her pussy clamp down on her fingers. Meadow muffled her scream with her hand as her orgasm slammed into her.

Sage gripped her ass, holding her in place as she rode the waves of her orgasm. She lapped up Meadow's release with her tongue, loving the taste of her mate. She could spend hours with her tongue buried inside of Meadow's pussy.

That was her version of heaven.

"So, have I told you how much I missed you?" Sage smiled as she pulled back from Meadow's delicious pussy. She just couldn't get enough. Her tongue gave one long swipe to Meadow's pussy. She sighed, realizing that she couldn't stay down here all day. With one more flick, she pulled back.

Meadow shuddered one last time and barked out a laugh. She dropped her leg down and leaned down, crushing her mouth to Sage's. They shared a deep passionate kiss before Meadow pulled back.

"Oh yes. You just told me." Meadow grinned at her. "I heard you loud and clear."

CHAPTER FIVE

"I was thinking that we could go out together," Meadow suggested. She bit her lip as she came from her shower. The last couple of weeks had been magical with Sage, though they hadn't put a label to their relationship. The few times that they'd been in public, most people just assumed that they were friends hanging out.

Meadow was ready for more.

Meadow wasn't sure what this was between them, but she was biting at the bit to announce to the world that they were lovers, not friends.

She wrapped her towel around her body as she crossed her bedroom and stood at the foot of the bed.

"Sure. What did you have in mind? We're supposed to go on the run tonight with a few pack members," Sage mentioned as she sat up on the bed. Having come in her wolf form, when she shifted, it left her naked. Not that Meadow minded at all. It was just that right now, she was trying to have a serious conversation with her and her plump mounds and beaded nipples were a big distraction.

"What is this between us?" she asked softly. She pushed her hair behind her ear as she stood at the edge of the bed.

Were they lovers? Were they friends who just happened to have sex with each other? Were they each other's mates? Meadow believed deep down that Sage was the one for her. Her wolf believed it, but she didn't know if Sage recognized her as her mate.

"Meadow," Sage sighed as she crawled toward the edge of the bed.

"Stop." Meadow raised her hand, causing Sage to pause in the middle of the bed. She sat down and looked to Meadow. "When you come near me, I lose all train of thought. I just want to know what this is between us. Are we lovers? Are we friends that have a healthy sex life—"

"Meadow." Sage's quiet stare made her heart race. Meadow couldn't read her when she erased all emotions from her face. It was like she had shifted into her enforcer mode.

Meadow paused and looked to Sage. Her

stomach rolled with the thought that this would be how Sage would decide to end whatever this was between them. She'd tried not to seem clingy or anything. Her wolf paced as she waited for Sage to speak.

"Meadow, I would love nothing more than to scream to the world and our pack that we're lovers. Girlfriends if you want to put a label on it. I wasn't sure if you were ready for that step," Sage said quietly. Her face softened as she motioned for Meadow to join her on the bed.

"Really?" Relief filled her as she hopped onto the bed. She crawled across and knelt before Sage. "You want the world to know that we're lovers?"

"Yes," Sage growled, snagging the front of her towel and pulling it off of her. She tossed the offending material to the floor. Meadow dove toward Sage, knocking them back on the bed.

"Oh, Sage, that makes me feel better," she murmured as she covered her lips with hers. Their kiss deepened with an urgency. "I wish I would have said something before."

"You should always feel comfortable talking with me." Sage placed a chaste kiss to her lips. A small smile spread across her face as she glanced down at Meadow. "So, will you go on the pack run tonight as my girlfriend?"

ARIEL MARIE

"Are you asking me out on a date?" Meadow play-fully batted her eyes at Sage.

"You're damn right I am," Sage growled, crushing her lips to Meadow's, sliding her tongue inside. Meadow wrapped her arms around Sage's neck, pulling her close. Their breasts rubbed together as they became lost in each other. Meadow could feel herself grow aroused from their shared kiss.

She turned her pleasure over to Sage as she normally did. Sage smiled at her as she knelt in between her legs. Meadow's core pulsed with just Sage glancing down her valley below.

"I want you," Meadow murmured as Sage grabbed her legs. A shiver ran along her spine as Sage ran her hands up her legs, bringing them up in the air.

"You have me." Sage placed a small kiss on her calf before she pushed Meadow's legs back to the bed. She settled herself onto Meadow where their two clits could join together.

Meadow gasped as Sage shifted, rubbing her slick pussy against hers. This had to be one of her favorite positions for Sage to take her. No matter how many times they had made love, with just them or with toys, this was her favorite. It was the most intimate position where their two moist pussies could slide against each other. Their juices would run together, mixing and coating both of them in the evidence of their lovemaking.

She cried out as her swollen clit rubbed against Sage's as she began to rock against her.

"Sage," Meadow gasped her lover's name. Their eyes connected as Sage began to thrust her clit against Meadow's. Sage picked up her speed, grabbing one of Meadow's legs as she leaned over her. She reached up and grabbed Sage's breast and latched onto it, sucking it deep into her mouth. Her hands made their way to Sage's ass, pulling her close to allow her to grind her pussy against her lover's.

Sage cried out as Meadow nipped her breast. She let it go as her cries joined Sage's, filling the air. Sage rode her hard, and she could feel their juices running in between them. The sound of their coupling echoed through the air and was proof enough that they were enjoying each other.

"Fuck! Meadow!" Sage cried out as Meadow latched onto her other breast. She sucked on it, trying to fit as much of the mound into her mouth as possible. They both thrust against each other fast and hard, both close to orgasm.

"Sage, come here." She popped the breast from her mouth and pulled Sage to her. Their mouths fused together as they continued to thrust against each other.

She gripped Sage's ass in her hand, helping her grind her swollen clit against hers.

Sage thrust her tongue deep in her mouth. Their tongues dueled together as their lovemaking grew frantic.

"Come with me," Sage cried out against her lips. Their bodies trembled in unison as they cried out their releases. Meadow threw back her head as she screamed her release. Her fangs broke through her gums and it took everything she had not to sink her teeth into Sage.

Biting during lovemaking would symbolize a claiming, and her wolf ached to claim Sage, but not now.

Her breaths were coming fast as she opened her eyes and found Sage staring at her.

"The run is in about an hour," Sage murmured, slowly moving her pussy from against Meadow's sensitive clit. She gasped at Sage's teasing methods.

"Okay," Meadow sighed, reaching up to run her fingers through Sage's dark tresses. She loved everything about the woman who had made her orgasm more times than anyone had before her. Her hands gently trailed along her back and down to her firm ass cheeks. "We're still going, right?"

Meadow shifted her legs, bringing them down and locking her ankles together beneath Sage's ass. She didn't want her lover to move from her position on top of her. Sage rolled them to their side, shifting their bodies to where she cradled Meadow to her.

"Of course. What I was going to say is that I don't want us to shower as we've been doing. If we're going let people know about us, then we're going all-out. I want them to be able to scent not just me on you, I want them to scent my pussy on you," Sage murmured against her lips.

Meadow smiled, having no argument to the request. Her heart literally jumped for joy as she pulled Sage's face to hers.

"Well, if that's the case, let's get your pussy on me properly." She shifted her body to allow her to straddle Sage's face and put Sage's pussy in hers.

"I like the way you think, my sexy little school teacher," Sage murmured, wasting no time thrusting her tongue in between Meadow's slick folds.

Meadow pushed her lover's legs apart and smiled. "Just you wait, I have more ideas."

She lowered her head and covered Sage's pussy with her mouth. She growled deep in her chest as her tongue went on an exploration mission to find Sage's clit.

Yes, she had plenty more ideas for them.

One that included making their relationship official.

Sage pulled Meadow close to her as they walked through the forest. It was late, and it was the perfect time to go for a pack run. This run was just for those needing to stretch out their animal legs and let them run loose. Each month, the pack did one run with the alpha and the enforcers. Other runs were organized for anyone who wanted to get out and socialize their animals.

"I just want you to know that I wasn't trying to pressure you or anything," Meadow said as they made it close to the meeting destination.

She stopped and pulled Meadow to face her. The thick woods provided them privacy. With her shifter vision, she could see the apprehension on Meadow's face. She smiled as she reached up a hand and cupped Meadow's jaw. Their bodies automatically moved closer to each other. She traced Meadow's jawline with her finger, tipping her chin up to where she could look down into her mate's eyes.

"*Mate,*" her animal whispered.

She smiled, because deep in her heart she knew it to be true. Meadow was the only person in the world that made her heart race, made her core clench with just one look, and made her feel whole. She was in love with this woman in front of her, and she would make sure that she proved it to her. Her wolf pawed at her chest, ready to get out to mingle with Meadow's wolf.

"I want to be with you," she murmured, gazing deep into Meadow's eyes. "I told you that I want everyone to know that you belong to me. These lips belong to me." She leaned in and pressed her lips to Meadow's in a slow, deep kiss. She gripped the back of Meadow's head as she angled her head to deepen the kiss. Her tongue swept inside of Meadow's mouth, tasting her mate. She pulled back and placed a smaller kiss on Meadow's lips.

Meadow's eyes slowly opened as Sage ran her finger down her neck toward her perky breasts. Her hands gripped Meadow's large mounds.

"Sage," Meadow gasped, her breath coming fast.

"These beautiful breasts belong in my mouth," Sage whispered. Meadow's body leaned into hers as she wrapped her arms around her. Her hands slid down to the supple curve of Meadow's ass, pulling her against her. Her little whimper caused Sage's beast to claw at her insides, trying to break free. "So don't doubt me, Meadow. I want you and I want the whole world to know it."

Meadow's hot breath blew on Sage's neck as she nestled her face against Sage's.

"I want you too, Sage," Meadow whispered. Sage knew that they were sliding down the slippery slope of lust. Any more and she'd rip their clothes off and take Meadow right there in the woods. There was no telling who else was walking near them to get to the meeting place. Her wolf was a jealous wolf, and she didn't want anyone to see Meadow's luscious body.

"Not right now, my love," she whispered, pulling back and away from Meadow. The scent of their arousals floated through the air. She groaned as she looked at Meadow's kiss swollen lips. Unable to resist, she kissed Meadow again. "I promise you as soon as we get back, you can have me any way you want."

"Promise?"

"You better believe it. Now, let's go meet the others." Sage grabbed Meadow's hand and pulled her along behind her. Her wolf whined, ready to break free. She was ready to run through the forest with the other members of the pack.

They came into the clearing where members of the pack where gathered amongst themselves, deep in conversation. The voices paused as everyone took in their entwined hands. Meadow tightened her grip on Sage's hand as they stood facing the group. She tucked Meadow under her arm and guided her toward the crowd. The voices resumed as people went back to their conversations.

It was official.

They were a couple.

CHAPTER SIX

"So you and the new school teacher?" Kortan asked as she took her spot at the table at the main house. They were having their monthly meeting with the enforcers and the Alpha.

She glanced at Kortan and couldn't keep the smile from forming on her lips. A few nights ago, when she and Meadow had showed up for the late run with a few of the pack members, the whispers had started. They had certainly made a statement. The twenty or so wolves that they shifted and ran with, were able to scent that Meadow had been with Sage. Her wolf had strutted around proudly, glad that their secret was finally out.

"Yes, sir." She smiled. "Meadow is amazing."

"I'm happy for you." Kortan nodded his head. Her

heart skipped a beat at her alpha's immediate acceptance of her relationship with Meadow. She didn't know why she would have thought that Kortan would have had a problem with it. His very own sister, Liberty, was mated to Lyric, another female.

The other enforcers began filing into the room, and her smile faded as they began discussing pack business. For the next hour, Kortan led the meeting. She glanced around the room, pride filling her chest that she was the first female enforcer of the Moon Valley pack.

"We need to ensure that we're keeping an eye on our borders," Kortan informed the room. "Rogues have been sighted in Ashton Hills. I've spoken with their alpha, and so far, the rogues have just passed through."

Sage's wolf stood at attention at the mention of rogues. They were not bound to any rules or laws that all wolf shifters abided by. They were the most dangerous kind of shifters, and this threat was serious.

"Did the alpha say which direction the rogues were moving in?" she asked. As an enforcer, it was their job to ensure that the townspeople of Moon Valley were kept safe.

"Coming in our direction. Let's hope they don't stop and keep going," Kortan replied. "I want you to partner up on patrols for the next week for safety measures."

Murmurs echoed through the room as everyone

began to disperse. Sage stood from the table, concern for their pack filling her chest. It was the job of the enforcers to ensure that the pack remained safe and secure.

"Hey, Sage," a deep voice called out. She turned to find Orion at her side. He was someone that she considered a friend. He had been one of the few guys that had accepted her immediately when she was selected as an enforcer. It wasn't that she couldn't trust her fellow enforcers, it just took a little time for the guys to warm up to a woman being on the team.

"Orion, what's up?"

"Want to be partners?" he asked, a grin plastered on his face.

"Of course," she chuckled, tucking a hair behind her ear.

"What time do you want to meet up? I figured we'd patrol the Northern quadrant."

The Northern quadrant included Meadow's cabin. She could stay with her until it was time for them to go on patrol.

"That'd be perfect." She smiled as they walked out of the room.

"I figured that you'd want that area since its closest to your girl's place."

"Wait, how did you—"

"You should know that word travels fast in a small

town such as Moon Valley. You and the little school teacher have been the talk of the town," he chuckled, holding the door open for her.

"Really?" her voice ended on a squeak. She knew that they both agreed to let the pack know, but she didn't realize that their little stunt at the pack run would let the *entire* pack know that they were together.

She chuckled, thinking of how the town gossips must have been going crazy.

"Yup. The entire town has been talking about you two," Orion informed her. "Hey, do you want a ride?"

"Nah. It's beautiful out, so I'm going to walk home. Thanks. Meet you at seven?"

"Yup, that's fine. See you later." Orion jogged off toward his pickup truck that was parked in the parking lot of the pack's main building.

Sage figured she'd walk to Meadow's house and surprise her. She had been given her own copy of the key so that she could always let herself in. She glanced down at her watch and saw that school should be letting out soon, and the walk to Meadow's house was a good ten minutes. She had a few hours before she was due to meet Orion and could think of plenty to do to fill her time.

She arrived at Meadow's cabin and jogged up the few stairs to her cabin. She paused as she stood before the front door and turned her head, catching the scent of another wolf.

Her wolf stood at attention as she walked back to the edge of the porch and looked around. She got an eerie feeling as she headed down the stairs and walked around the side of the house. Meadow's house was one of the more secluded ones in this area. She had shared with Sage that she'd picked this cabin out because of the seclusion and it being so close to the woods.

Someone had been on Meadow's property.

Sage quickly disrobed and let her animal forward. She fell to the ground as the change took her. Dark fur sprouted from her skin, and within seconds, she stood on four legs.

Her animal let loose a deep warning growl in case the trespasser was still close by. She trotted over to the edge of the property that was lined with bushes that acted as a barrier to the woods. Her nose began its job sniffing out the scents that floated around the edge of the woods, finding unfamiliar scents.

Could this be rogues, or just some kids playing in the forest? She took her time searching the land, but she came up empty-handed.

The sound of a car door slamming echoed through the air.

Meadow.

She trotted back toward the house to greet her

mate. Her eyes took in Meadow as she walked around her car, and a smile lit up her mate's face. Sage knew that she could no longer hide the secret.

Today would be the day that she'd ask Meadow to mate with her.

"Sage!" Meadow called out as her eyes took in Sage's wolf. "How'd you beat me here?"

Sage whined as they walked up the stairs to the cabin. Meadow had on a sexy dress that flowed around her knees, highlighting all of her curves. Sage followed behind Meadow as she opened the door.

Her wolf wanted to stay a little longer, but Sage needed to return to her human form. She needed to greet her mate properly. She pulled back on her animal, allowing the change to take her.

"I missed you," Sage breathed as she stood from her spot on the floor. She stalked toward Meadow, pushing her up against the front door. She could see the impression of Meadow's nipples pushing against the material. She breathed deep and found her mate to be aroused.

"I couldn't help but think of our little rendezvous in my storage room the other day." Meadow smiled at Sage as she pushed her naked form against her body.

"Really? And what were you thinking about?" Sage's hands slid beneath Meadow's dress. She grabbed hold of the tiny scrap of material that acted as panties and pulled them down. "When was this?"

"On my lunch break today. I was in there putting some toys away, and the memories came back to me as I was in the storage room while the kids were at their lunch and recess. I shut the door and I couldn't help myself."

Her wide, innocent eyes gazed into Sage's. A smile graced Sage's lips as she reached behind Meadow and unzipped her dress. It fell in a pool of material on the floor, leaving Meadow in just her bra. Sage didn't want anything covering Meadow's body. It was perfect and curvy, and it was a shame to have to cover it up.

"And what did the little naughty teacher do while she was in the closet?" Sage guided Meadow over to the couch and pushed her down on the oversized furniture. She took a seat on the ottoman that was in front of the couch, giving her a front row seat to her mate's performance.

"I touched myself," Meadow whispered. She slowly ran her fingers down her naked body, all the while spreading her legs. Sage groaned at the sight of Meadow's fingers parting her own folds.

"Show me what you did," Sage murmured, feeling excitement lining her chest. Her mate's small fingers disappeared into her wet channel. Her keen shifter sight caught the sticky wetness on her fingers as she pulled them out. Unable to resist, Sage leaned forward and captured those fingers in her mouth. The taste of her mate caused her to groan in ecstasy.

"Let me show you," Meadow chuckled, withdrawing her fingers from Sage's lips. She slid her fingers back to her pussy and parted her labia, putting her clitoris on display. It was engorged and deep rose in color.

Sage's heart rate increased as she watched Meadow introduce her other hand to help. Her breaths were coming fast as she watched Meadow flick her clit with the new fingers. Her soft moans filled the air as she continued to pleasure herself in front of Sage. Her hips thrust forward to push her pussy forward.

Sage's pussy ached to have Meadow's tongue deep within her folds. She could feel the wetness slide down her thighs as she watched her mate begin to finger fuck herself.

"Sage," Meadow moaned.

Sage snapped.

She needed to have the taste of her mate on her tongue. She wanted to be the reason why Meadow screamed to the high heavens. She wanted to drink in her mate's release.

"I need you, Meadow," she growled, moving over Meadow. She slid her hands to Meadow's drenched pussy and thrust two fingers inside of her easily. Meadow's wetness immediately coated Sage's fingers. Her fingers slid in and out of her mate easily, thanks to her arousal.

She crushed her mouth to Meadow's, drinking in her moans. Meadow's muscles contracted around her fingers, letting her know that her mate was close to orgasm. Their nipples grazed each other's as the kiss deepened. Sage curled her fingers around to where she could rub Meadow's clit with her thumb, eliciting a deep moan.

"Sage, please. Make me come," Meadow gasped, tearing her lips from Sage's.

"As my mate wishes," she murmured, trailing her tongue down Meadow's body. She made pit stops at both of her breasts. Meadow's nipples were hard and thrust up into the air. She suckled them both deep into her mouth, taking the time to lick, nip, and suck them both. A snarl formed from deep within her chest as she made her way down Meadow's body. Her sweet scent of arousal greeted her as she became eye level with her drenched core. The evidence of her arousal was on her thighs.

Sage took her time, leaving kisses on Meadow's thighs as she kissed everywhere but her pussy.

"Stop teasing me," Meadow commanded, her voice ending on a growl.

Sage chuckled as she traced the glistening labia with her finger.

"There's no use in rushing a good thing, my love," she murmured, sliding her fingers deep into her again. Meadow's labia was swollen and puckered. Her clit pushed through the slit, as if demanding attention. Sage was only too happy to oblige, covering her entire pussy with her mouth.

Meadow's back arched off the couch as she feasted on her mate's sweet pussy. She used her fingers and spread Meadow's lips wide so that she could lick all of Meadow's pink goodness.

Meadow's juices were flowing freely from her pussy as Sage continued to lick her slit and trail her tongue up to flick her clitoris unmercifully. Sage repeatedly thrust her fingers into Meadow's tight channel.

Her muscles tightened and she screamed as she exploded. Her body tried to buck Sage off, but she held on, not letting go of her mate's pussy. She shook her head and hummed her pleasure that her mate climaxed so hard. She continued to drink Meadow's release as her body flopped back onto the couch.

Sage crawled back up Meadow's body and laid on her side, bringing Meadow's relaxed body flush against hers where they were facing each other. Their nipples molded against each other. They laid there, both out of breath. Sage's pussy tingled, wanting to release, but right now, it was all about Meadow.

CHAPTER SEVEN

Meadow smiled as she moved through her home. Sage had left to go on patrol with her partner. She worried slightly that there were rogues in the area. She knew that Moon Valley was safe under Kortan's watch, and she was confident that the alpha wouldn't let rogues into the town.

She couldn't help the grin that spread across her face as she thought of Sage using the term of mate during their lovemaking on the couch. They would have much to talk about once Sage returned from her patrol.

Meadow entered the kitchen, wanting to be a good little mate for Sage and make sure dinner was done when she returned. She bustled around the kitchen, grabbing what she needed to make a dinner worthy of discussing mating. They didn't get to talk about it, but Sage informed her before she left that they had something important to discuss. Her partner had showed up early, causing Sage to leave earlier than expected.

She hummed a song as she prepared the food. She glanced out the window over the sink as she washed her hands. The sun had gone down, leaving the back yard in darkness, but her eyes picked up movement in the yard.

"What the hell?" she murmured as she stared out the window.

Sage couldn't have returned that quick.

Meadow shut the water off and grabbed the drying tool from the counter and dried her hands. She moved toward the back door and saw something run past the back steps.

Her wolf growled low in her chest, wanting to protect her territory.

"It was probably a stray dog," she whispered, opening the door. She stepped out onto the back porch and didn't hear anything. She looked up at the moon and smiled as she walked down the few stairs and stood on the last one. She sniffed, and automatically picked up a new scent that was unfamiliar.

Her animal slammed against her chest, warning her. She took a step back as her eyes locked on three massive wolves appearing at the edge of the woods.

Rogues.

Growls filled the air as she backed her way up the stairs, not daring to take her eyes off the advancing wolves. She backed up into a hard figure and let loose a scream.

"Where do you think you're going, pretty lady?" a hard voice asked, as two large hands gripped her arms. The rough hands turned her, putting her face to face with a naked rogue.

"Let me go and leave," she threatened. "My mate is an enforcer and will be back any moment."

He pulled her forward, thrusting his face into the crook of her neck. She fought to free herself, but he was too strong for her. His musty scent filled her nostrils, causing her to gag.

"Ain't no male been intimate with this little lady here," he called out to the other wolves. "She's got the smell of another female's pussy on her."

"Stop!" she growled, trying to break free from his grasp. He flipped her around, bringing her back to his naked front. She cried out as she felt his hardened length brush her pants. "Let me go!"

"Looks like we found the perfect house, boys!" he called out, chuckling. "Two females hot for each other."

A wolf's howl could be heard echoing through the woods. His grip tightened on her as his friends stopped at the base of the stairs. They turned and planted their paws as they gazed around the yard. Their growls filled the air as they waited.

"Help me!" she cried out, before the rogue slapped his hand across her mouth.

"Go ahead and cry out for your female lover," he breathed in her ear. "Once she gets here, me and my wolves will have some fun with the both of you."

Tears filled her eyes as she frantically searched for Sage. She prayed she didn't come by herself. There was no way that she'd be able to take on four rogue wolves alone.

His sadistic laugh filled the air as a single wolf appeared in the clearing. Meadow shook her head, recognizing Sage's wolf. She wanted to scream for her to run away, but the rogue still held his hand across her mouth.

"Well, look what we have here, the other female. Looks like we're having fun tonight, boys," he hollered.

The three wolves advanced slowly on Sage. She bared her fangs, not backing down from the wolves.

Meadow didn't know if her mate was brave or just downright crazy.

"She's a fighter, isn't she?" he snarled, yanking on Meadow's shirt. She cried out as her body was jostled in his arms as he exposed her bra-clad chest. Tears burned down her face as she cried out. "Let's show her what she's going to be fighting for."

"Run!" she screamed to Sage. She didn't want her to get caught by the rogues. She wrestled with the rogue who had her, but he gripped her around her neck with his forearm.

"You're not going anywhere," he growled, his lips brushing against her ear.

A deep howl echoed strong through the air. This one louder and filled with power.

The alpha.

The wolves grew skittish as a dozen or so wolves crept from the woods.

The pack enforcers and the alpha appeared.

Kortan was larger than the enforcers. His wolf was menacing as it stepped next to Sage.

The rogue holding Meadow threw her to the ground with a curse as he jumped down the stairs.

Meadow attempted to pull her shirt together as she watched the rogue who held her shift back to his wolf form. Sage and the pack advanced on the rogues.

Meadow watched as Sage went after the wolf that assaulted her. Her wolf snarled, wanting to break free and fight, but she knew the enforcers would take care of the rogues. She watched as the rogues were driven away from her property and disappeared into the woods with the enforcers right behind them.

Meadow scrambled from her feet as the fight moved deeper into the woods. She could hear growls and snarls echoing through the air. She took a few steps and her legs gave way, causing her to fall to the ground.

"Meadow!" Sage called out, jogging from the woods in her human form. She raced across the yard, naked from her shift. She knelt next to Meadow and gently cupped her jaw, bringing her eyes up to meet hers. "Are you all right?"

"I was so scared," Meadow whimpered, reaching for Sage. She gripped Sage to her, thankful that nothing had happened to her. Images of what could have happened crossed her mind and she tightened her grip.

"You're safe now. Kortan and the rest of the enforcers have dealt with the rogues. They can't bother anyone else, ever," Sage growled against the top of Meadow's head.

"I was afraid for you. I didn't want you to be hurt going against three wolves."

"I'm flattered that you would be worried about me, but I'm an enforcer. This is what I do," Sage chuckled, pushing the hair from Meadow's face.

"It's a little scarier seeing it in action." She knew that Sage was an enforcer and it was nothing like seeing her mate facing three vicious rogues that gave her a rude wakeup call of how dangerous the job truly was. She turned her eyes to Sage and knew that it was time. "Mate with me."

Sage's eyes widened at first, before a smile broke out on her face. She pulled Meadow up to her feet and pulled her body flush against hers.

"That was going to be my line," Sage chuckled. "But the answer is yes."

CHAPTER EIGHT

"Once you're there, you'll know it." Libby smiled at Sage, and she smiled back at her alpha's sister. Lyric and Libby beamed as they held hands before Sage and Meadow. When Sage had asked permission for her and Meadow to take the final leap into mating, she had been worried briefly that the alpha wouldn't do it.

Just because he did it for his sister and her mate, didn't mean that he'd do it for her and Meadow. But she should have known better. Kortan was a fair alpha, and he didn't hesitate in agreeing to her request.

"Once the trees break open to the moonlight, you will see your gift," Lyric said with a cheesy grin on her face.

"Thank you so much." Meadow grabbed Sage's hand and pulled her to the woods.

"Meadow, that was rude." Sage laughed as they entered into the thick woods.

"Well, they know I didn't mean to be rude, but I'm ready to claim my mate," Meadow giggled as she pulled Sage behind her.

Sage sighed as she followed behind her lover. In just a short time, she had fallen madly in love with the sexy school teacher. Her wolf paced inside her chest, knowing that shortly they would be claiming Meadow and her wolf. She could feel her gums burn as her eyes caught the gentle sway of Meadow's ass as she followed her.

"It shouldn't be too much longer," Sage murmured as she took in their surroundings. They walked in a comfortable silence in the direction that Lyric and Libby mentioned. She wasn't quite sure what the two had come up with for her and Meadow.

"Oh, Sage," Meadow gasped, coming to a complete halt. Sage bumped into Meadow, her arms automatically encircling her mate. She glanced over her shoulder and took in the cozy little oasis of blankets and pillows that lay before them. She smiled, thinking of how romantic it was, and squeezed Meadow to her as she leaned her chin on Meadow's shoulder.

"We definitely have to thank Libby and Lyric." Her lips brushed against the curve of Meadow's neck.

"Yes, we'll have to make sure they're on our

Christmas card list," Meadow breathed as Sage ran her sharp fangs along the delicate skin. Her hands inched their way up Meadow's stomach until they cupped her oversized breasts.

A groan escaped Meadow as Sage nipped her skin. She pressed her aching breasts against Meadow's back, her wolf demanding that they claim their mate.

Meadow's aroused scent floated through the air, causing Sage to let loose a deep growl. Meadow tilted her head back and their lips met in a passionate kiss. Sage's hand shifted slightly to allow her claws to burst forth and sliced Meadow's dress from her body.

Meadow tore her mouth from Sage's with a gasp.

"Sage!" Her lips tilted up in the corner as the tattered shreds of her dress floated to the ground. Sage's hand returned to that of her human hand as she gripped her mate's naked flesh.

"Someone's a naughty girl," she chucked as her hands ran along Meadow's curvy body, finding her completely nude.

"And someone has entirely too many clothes on," Meadow quipped, turning around in Sage's arms.

"I'm sure we can rectify that." Sage captured Meadow's lips with hers. Meadow's hands slid along her shoulders as she pulled Sage to her. A growl vibrated in her chest as Meadow threaded her fingers in Sage's hair.

Her hands slid down and filled themselves with Meadow's plump ass. She burned a trail of kisses along Meadow's jawline and down her neck. She took a step forward, making Meadow step back, and the sounds of fabric tearing filled the air as Meadow ripped Sage's shirt from her body, leaving her in her shorts and bra.

"I want you naked now," Meadow pouted.

"In time," Sage murmured, pushing Meadow down onto the mound of blankets. Meadow shrieked as she tumbled down onto the bed. She paused as she took in the sight of her mate laying on the blankets with her legs spread wide.

"Join me, mate." Meadow beckoned Sage with her fingers, her eyes drawn to Meadow's core. She could scent the strong arousal that was filling the air. She quickly disrobed and knelt on the makeshift bed.

"I love you, Meadow," Sage purred as she let her fingers trace along Meadow's legs. Her eyes met Meadow's as she moved closer, in between her spread legs.

"I love you too, mate," Meadow murmured. Her hooded eyes were locked on Sage as she continued to run her hands along her toned legs.

Her hands ran along Meadow's skin, meeting at her bare mons pubis. A quick intake of breath let her know that Meadow was affected by her exploration. She trailed her hands along Meadow's belly and up to her breasts. Sage leaned over her mate, unable to resist tasting them. Her mouth captured Meadow's right nipple in between her lips. She sucked more of the breast into her mouth as she settled her body into the valley of Meadow's thighs.

"Sage," Meadow moaned, her fingers threading their way into her hair, holding Sage to her breast.

She loved the sound of her name on her mate's lips. She shifted her body to allow her hand to slide down Meadow's body. She parted Meadow's labia with her fingertips, sliding in between the slick folds. Meadow's slick heat coated her fingers as she explored her mate's pussy. She knew what her mate liked and what made her moan.

She slid two fingers deep within Meadow's core. The tight muscular walls clamped down on Sage's fingers as she thrust them deep. She used her thumb to tease Meadow's swollen clitoris as she continued to thrust her fingers.

"You belong to me," she growled, letting Meadow's breast go. She shifted her body to allow their lips to meet in a crushing kiss, increasing the pace of her fingers as they pounded into Meadow's slick core.

"Yes," Meadow hissed, throwing her head back. Sage's eyes locked in on Meadow's neck as she turned her head away from Sage. Her breasts brushed against Meadow's as she licked her way to Meadow's neck.

The mating call gripped her as she bathed Meadow's neck with her tongue. Meadow's hips thrust forward, meeting her fingers for every thrust. Meadow's breaths were coming fast, as were Sage's. She knew her mate was close to her orgasm. She was turned on by the simple fact that she was bringing such pleasure to Meadow.

"Sage," Meadow cried out, her body writhing beneath hers as her muscles tightened. Her body arched with a long, drawn-out cry as she reached her peek. Sage sank her fangs into Meadow's shoulder, and stars exploded behind Sage's closed eyes. She could feel the link between her and Meadow sink into place.

The taste of Meadow's blood filled her mouth. She pulled back with a howl, announcing she had claimed her mate. Meadow turned and grabbed her neck. She threw her leg over Sage and tossed her weight to change their positions.

Meadow straddled Sage with a small smile on her lips.

"My turn," she growled, before sinking her fangs into Sage's neck.

Meadow licked the wound, ensuring that the bleeding was controlled.

They were officially mated in the eyes of their wolves.

She trailed her tongue down Sage's body from her neck to her breasts. She made pit stops along the way, and made sure that she paid both of Sage's mounds attention. Sage's breasts were the sweetest that she'd ever tasted.

"I love the way your breasts fit in my mouth," Meadow murmured against her skin. She lathed the nipple with her tongue before moving further down. The scent of Sage's arousal called to her. She needed to have the taste of Sage's delicious heat on her tongue.

"I love you and your talented little tongue." Meadow chuckled as she continued her journey.

She settled into the valley of Sage's legs with her eyes level with her mate's slick labia. Sage's pussy was perfect. Her small labia was swollen with need, hiding her bundle of nerves. She covered Sage's pussy with her mouth, sucking in all the moisture that had gathered on it. Sage's legs widened to give her full access to her pussy. Meadow parted her mate's sweet labia with her tongue, gathering all of her nectar. She moaned as the taste of Sage exploded on her tongue.

She grabbed Sage's legs as her tongue made its way to her buried bundle of nerves, her tongue connecting with Sage's clit. She sucked it deep into her mouth as Sage thrust. She smiled, slipping her fingers deep into

Sage's slick opening as she focused on her clit. She repeatedly thrust her fingers deep within her mate as she sucked, pulled, and licked the nub.

"Meadow!" Sage cried out as she refused to let up on her mate. She wanted to return the favor and make Sage fall apart. She turned and arched her fingers inside of Sage and found that certain spot that she knew would make her mate fly off into the heavens.

Sage's scream echoed through the night. Meadow basked in the joy of her making her mate have such a strong orgasm. She buried her tongue deep within her mate's folds, licking up all of her release.

Sage's body settled down on their makeshift bed. Meadow climbed back over her mate and braced herself over her. She gazed down at her mate with her eyes closed, trying to catch her breath. She loved this woman more than life itself, and could not wait to see what the future held for them.

Sage opened her eyes and they gazed lovingly at each other. She leaned down and covered her mouth with hers, and knew that this was just the beginning.

EPILOGUE

Sage gripped Meadow's hand tight as she led her from the woods. Their mating would continue with the acceptance of the pack and the show of their mating marks. Sage strode with pride with Meadow by her side.

Eyes of the entire pack turned their way as the two of them walked across the small clearing. The crowd parted as Kortan stepped forward. Sage smiled at her alpha as she and Meadow came to a halt in front of him. His eyes went to their mating marks and he gave them both a nod.

Once he announced them as a couple in front of the entire pack, everyone would shift and go on a pack run.

Meadow tightened her grip on her hand, causing her to glance over at her.

"I love you," Meadow murmured, leaning against her arm. She wrapped her arm around Meadow and pulled her close.

"I love you too," she murmured against Meadow's head.

"Moon Valley," Kortan called out, gaining the attention of the entire pack.

Tonight would be their very first pack run as an officially mated couple. Sage's chest filled with pride at the thought of being able to call Meadow her mate.

"Two more of our own have found their destined mates. Both are prominent members of our community, and I offer my blessing to them." He moved to stand behind them.

"Have they marked each other?" someone called out.

"That they have," he replied.

They both turned their necks to show their freshly made mating marks that would forever show that they belonged to each other. This time, it was Sage who squeezed the hand of Meadow. This was the moment that they had been waiting for.

To be accepted as a mated couple by their pack.

"Are there any here tonight who would object to the mating of these two?" Kortan called out. He placed his hands on their shoulders as they waited for any objections.

Sage's eyes roamed the crowd, and she caught sight of Libby and Lyric smiling at her. She mouthed, "thank you" to them for the beautiful little corner of heaven that they had created for them to officially mate.

"It would seem that there are no objections to the mating of two wonderful females of our pack. Meadow and Sage, may you have a wonderful, long life, full of love."

Sage turned to Meadow and pulled her to her. She covered her mouth for a short passionate kiss. Claps and whistles filled the air from their pack. Sage pulled back from Meadow and rested her forehead against hers. She couldn't think of a better person to share her life with.

From this day forward, they would have an eternity together as mates.

TUESDAY'S MATE

Moon Valley Shifters

Book 3

CHAPTER ONE

Tuesday Webb gazed around her small office with great pride. She had recently moved to of Moon Valley, a town that had attracted her because it was a close-knit shifter community, had a thriving economy, and it had a reputation as an up-and-coming town for young wolves to settle in.

Her small accounting business would be the only one in the small town, and she knew that she could capitalize on that alone. Her smile grew just thinking of her future here in Moon Valley.

She walked out to her small receptionist area and waiting room. She would have to find a secretary soon. To try to give the waiting area a more homey feeling, she had placed a few magazines on the coffee table that sat by the chairs where clients would wait. Thankfully, the alpha's secretary, Pola, offered to help her until she could get someone full-time.

That in itself was why she loved this town already. The members pulled together and helped each other out. Where she was from, she would have just been on her own until she hired someone. The town of Bristol was just a lot larger than Moon Valley and everyone was about themselves. Her mother just didn't understand completely why Tuesday wanted to leave the safety of a town she had grown up in, but Tuesday had decided that if she wanted to make a good life for herself, she'd have to take the chance and go after her dreams.

And that included a successful career and finding a mate to settle down with.

She'd moved to Moon Valley and hadn't looked back since.

This morning, she'd called the local newspaper and paid to have an ad run for a receptionist. Tuesday crossed her fingers that it wouldn't take long to get someone to fill the position.

Her stomach let loose a growl and she glanced down at her watch.

"Okay already." She laughed, not realizing that time had gotten away from her since she'd arrived at the office. Her wolf growled too, putting in her two cents. "Okay, I get it. We're hungry."

She chuckled as she walked back into her office and grabbed her wristlet with her cash in it. There was a cute little coffee shop a few doors down that she could run and grab a bite to eat at before she finished unpacking her office. She even grabbed a few of her business cards. She could use this as an opportunity to drum up some business for herself.

She quickly stepped out of her office and locked the door, tossing her cards in her wristlet.

"Good morning!" a small voice called out. Tuesday turned and caught sight of a small female waving to her. She searched her brain, and thankfully remembered her name. She'd remembered meeting her the weekend that she first moved to the town and now her name was escaping her.

"Morning. Lyric, isn't it?" she asked with a smile, as she tucked her thick blonde hair behind her ear.

"Yes. How's Moon Valley treating you so far?" Lyric asked, walking toward her.

"So far, so good."

"That's great! You'll love it here." Lyric's wide smile instantly made Tuesday feel welcomed. "I moved here last summer and fell in love with the town."

"That's great to hear. I was so nervous about moving here," Tuesday admitted.

"Well, if you ever want to grab a bite to eat, me and

ARIEL MARIE

my mate, Libby, would love to get together with you and introduce you around to the pack."

"Really?" she gasped. She was both surprised and thankful. It really warmed her heart that so many people were going out of their way to make sure she felt welcomed. Moon Valley had sunk its fangs in her and was becoming a part of her. She would not pass up on this opportunity to try and make new friends. "I would love that."

It would do her some good to get to know the pack. She'd went to the monthly pack meeting the weekend she'd moved to town and met a few people, but hadn't had time to get back out and meet more of the pack.

"Just let me know and I can arrange a girl's night out or a luncheon. Sorry to rush off, but I have to get to work. Libby doesn't tolerate a late assistant!" She winked as she waved and scurried down the hallway toward her office.

"I will, thanks!" Tuesday waved and turned, making her way out of the building. It was amazing that two females could be happily mated in this town without having to be harassed or looked down upon because they loved the same sex. It was comforting to know that the town allowed everyone to just be themselves.

Off to find breakfast, she exited the front door of the main building and smiled. Such a beautiful day.

The sun was bright and beat down on her bare shoulders. It was unusually warm for nine in the morning, but Tuesday wasn't going to complain. Summer was her favorite time of year. Her summer dress would help keep her cool and allow her to get some sun while she walked down the street.

Her wolf picked up on the scent of fresh coffee and pastries. She smiled at a few pedestrians before making her way to the Little Bean Café. She opened the door and was blasted with the fresh aroma of coffee beans and sweet delights.

Her wolf let loose a deep growl of pleasure as she pushed forward against Tuesday's chest. Tuesday had to push her animal down as she walked into the trendy café.

"Okay, we're here," she grumbled to herself. The café had a few customers in line before Tuesday, which was fine with her. It gave her time to study the menu that was posted on the wall behind the counter. Everything sounded good, and she was going to have a hard time deciding on what she wanted.

A sweet, flowery scent greeted her nostrils and her wolf stood at attention. She tore her eyes off the menu so that she could discover who the scent belonged to. Her wolf paced, taking notice of the scent, demanding that she find the other wolf.

Tuesday's eyes roamed the people in line in front

of her and dismissed them. The scent didn't belong to any of them. Disappointed, her eyes turned to the people working behind the counter, and her eyes fell on a woman with dark brown hair grabbing a pastry from the display case. Her breath caught in her throat as she took in the woman's extreme beauty.

The apron that she wore did nothing to hide her curves and large breasts. Tuesday was captivated by the woman as she worked on the orders for the customers before her. Her dark hair was pinned up in a messy bun on top of her head, and Tuesday ached to see what the thick hair would look like spread out on her bed sheets.

Her eyes widened at her thoughts.

She'd only been in town for two weeks, and finding a mate wasn't exactly on her mind, at least not yet. She'd wanted to get settled and make sure she got her business off the ground before she could even think of dating.

Large brown eyes met hers, and she realized that she'd been caught staring. Her cheeks grew warm from embarrassment, but she couldn't look away if she tried. Her nipples grew into taut little buds and pushed painfully against her thin summer dress. She watched as the woman's eyes dropped down and took notice of her breasts.

Her natural reaction would have been to cross her

arms against her chest to hide her reaction. But today, she was feeling a bit wanton so she stood up straighter, not wanting to hide her reaction as the woman looked her fill.

It felt amazing to have someone look at her with hunger in their eyes, just as the woman was looking at her now. She could feel her core clench as she felt the heat of the woman's gaze slowly glide down her body. She shifted in place as she waited for the woman's response. She bit her lip, and the woman's eyes darkened with approval as they came back up and met hers.

Tuesday smiled and glanced around to see if anyone had noticed the interaction between her and the female. The customer in front of her was too busy to notice, her attention totally consumed by her smartphone, and the other employees behind the counter were busy.

She moved up in line as the woman on her smartphone was being taken care of by one of the employees.

"Can I start making you something?" the woman asked, her eyes never leaving Tuesday. As she leaned over the display, Tuesday's eyes caught her nametag.

Sunni.

"Hello, Sunni," she murmured, glancing back up at the menu, having forgotten to make a decision on what she wanted. Thankfully, no one was behind her in line that she'd be holding up. "Um...this is my first time here. What would you recommend?"

A wide grin spread across Sunni's face as she winked at Tuesday. "Well, honey, considering I own the place, I'm a little biased. I think everything is good."

Tuesday giggled, tucking her hair behind her ear. She knew that the female was openly flirting with her and she loved it. Even her wolf was paying attention.

Tuesday tilted her head to the side, allowing her thick hair to tumble along her shoulder. She drew her lip in between her teeth, deciding there was nothing wrong with a little harmless flirting. Sunni's eyes dropped to her lips, and she knew that she had the woman's full attention.

"Well, if you're the owner, I'm sure there must be a secret menu that most customers don't know about." She cocked her eyebrow and waited. A smile played along her lips.

"Well, actually, there is." Sunni smiled, pushing off the counter. She turned and grabbed a laminated menu and handed it to her.

"I was just guessing." Tuesday laughed as she glanced at the menu. She wouldn't have expected a small café such as this to have a secret menu, but she was glad she had joked about it. She found a few things that sounded good and ordered one of them for now, and her coffee.

"Good choice." Sunni smiled before turning away to make up her order. Tuesday's day was continuing to look brighter. Before she left, she'd make sure that Sunni had her card. She'd be open to Sunni calling her for business or pleasure.

CHAPTER TWO

Sunni stared at the card that Tuesday had given her a few days ago. She'd called and spoke to Pola, who was currently helping the new accountant until she found a secretary. She'd made an appointment because it was great news that Moon Valley now had a resident accountant. Sunni hated having to travel to the next town just to have someone do her taxes and help with her business decisions.

Sunni wanted to get in with Tuesday before everyone started lining up at her door for advice. The town had been in need of a local accountant, and now they finally had one.

But there was the other reason why Sunni wanted to see the sexy accountant.

She was attracted to her.

The minute their eyes met, Sunni's wolf slammed into her chest. It had taken everything she had to not shift behind the counter and hop over it to get to Tuesday.

That would have been a sight.

She would certainly have scared the few humans in the restaurant. It wasn't that humans didn't know about shifters, it was just a little awkward if a person was making a cup of coffee and two seconds later, a large wolf was standing behind the counter with coffee spilled all over them.

She chuckled as she imagined what it would have looked like.

But Sunni was definitely ready to go meet with the new accountant.

This morning, Cindy, her lead barista, would be handling the opening of the Little Bean to allow Sunni to keep her appointment. Her employees were the best. They could run the place without her.

She stepped in front of her floor-length mirror to double check her outfit. It was mid-summer in Moon Valley, and it had been unreasonably warm lately. She didn't know what was going on with Mother Nature, but she needed to get her act together.

Her floor-length spaghetti strapped maxi dress would keep her cool. She'd left her thick hair down and tied it off to the side. It was too warm outside to have it end up plastered to her neck from sweating.

She wanted to look perfect for her appointment. Sunni had decided that she wanted the little wolf and she'd be going after her. What Sunni wanted, Sunni got. At the ripe age of twenty-eight, she wasn't getting any younger and was ready to find that special wolf to settle down with.

Shifters had the help of their animals to find their mates, and when Sunni's eyes landed on Tuesday, she was sure her wolf was close to screaming the "M" word.

Mate.

Satisfied with her look, she grabbed her messenger bag with all of her paperwork that she thought she would need for the appointment and headed out the door of her small apartment. Her place wasn't too far from her business, and she liked the closeness. She didn't even have to drive her car and could save on gas. She'd just enjoy the beautiful morning and walk to her appointment.

Ten minutes later, she was arriving at Tuesday's office. She stood outside and blew out a nervous breath.

"Maybe I should have brought her a coffee from the shop," she muttered to herself. Nothing like trying to bribe the new accountant to take her on as a client.

She glanced down at her watch and saw that she wouldn't have time. "Now or never."

She walked into the building with a smile as Pola came into view.

"Sunni, how are you?" Pola smiled from behind her desk.

"I'm doing well. How are you?" she asked, walking over to stand in front of the desk.

"I'm doing great. I think it's so awesome that Tuesday set up her practice here. Now you business owners won't have to go over to Pittsville to get your taxes done."

"I know," Sunni gushed. She was extremely happy to support a locally owned business. "I have an appointment with Tuesday."

"Yes, ma'am. She should be waiting for you." Pola gave Sunni instructions on where to find Tuesday's office. "Go in and have a seat in the reception area. I'll call her and let her know you're on your way."

"Thanks, Pola." Sunni waved and headed in the direction that Pola had given and made it to Tuesday's office. The sign on the door with Tuesday Webb, CPA etched in glass denoted that she had arrived at the correct office. She blew out a deep breath and brushed her slick hands on her dress.

She gripped the handle and turned, pushed the door open and strolled into the small waiting area that housed a few chairs, a coffee table, and the receptionist desk. She took a seat and rested her bag on her lap as she waited. Looking around, she could already see the personal touches.

Her wolf paced back and forth, sensing that they would be seeing Tuesday again. Her wolf had hounded her about Tuesday, and now they were only a few feet away from her.

Her attention was grabbed by the opening of the door behind the receptionist desk, and out walked Tuesday. Sunni's eyes were captivated by the wolf. Her blonde hair hung down around her shoulders in waves. She wore a flowery dress that stopped right at her knees, with a white blazer and heels that highlighted her toned calves.

"Sunni?" She smiled as she strolled toward Sunni with her outstretched hand.

"Tuesday. It's nice to see you again," she murmured, taking the accountant's hand. An electric current shot up her arm as their hands connected.

Mate.

The word was whispered in the back of her head and she smiled.

She knew it.

One of the reasons she loved being a shifter was that her animal could sense who she was to spend the rest of her life with. It made it much simpler than humans who searched forever, and then were not even sure that the person they married were to be with them forever.

A mating between shifters was forever.

And right now, her animal was identifying Tuesday as her mate.

"Thank you for stopping by." Tuesday motioned for Sunni to follow her into her office.

"No, thank you for taking me so soon." Sunni laughed as Tuesday closed the door behind them. She bit her lip to keep from moaning aloud as the scent of Tuesday hit her nostrils. Her wolf howled, loving the smell of Tuesday. Her sweet scent had Sunni wanting to bury her face in the crook of Tuesday's neck to be able to inhale the scent more. "You just don't know how much business you're about to get, being located here in Moon Valley."

"That's what I'm hoping for," Tuesday admitted, motioning for Sunni to take a seat in one of the chairs that faced her desk. "So, how can I help you?"

Sunni sat down and pulled her bag onto her lap. A quirky remark came to mind that she had to push down.

Down girl.

She reached into her bag and brought out a binder that she kept all of her records in. Tuesday sat in the chair next to hers and crossed her legs. She had to fight to keep from staring at the smooth skin of Tuesday's legs. Her wolf was just beneath her skin, sensing that Tuesday was near them. Her animal paced, demanding to be free. She wanted to meet Tuesday in person too.

"Well, being a small business owner and tax time just left us a few months ago, I just want to make sure that I'm going to be prepared for next year."

"Of course, I can help with that. It's good you want to be proactive. I can look over your books and make sure that you're taking advantage of deductions that are geared toward small business owners." Tuesday's bright smile met her as she took Sunni's portfolio. Her heart raced as she took in Tuesday's plump lips, and wondered if they were as sweet as they looked.

A fantasy of those lips covering her pussy came to mind and took her breath away.

Her body trembled with the thought.

She had to push thoughts like that down. She tried her best to keep her body from responding. She didn't want to come off as a horny little wolf; she was here for her business.

Not to get laid.

At least not at this second.

Her mind was made up. She was going to pursue the sexy accountant and make her hers.

Tuesday just didn't realize it yet.

Sunni relaxed as they began to go over the Little

Bean's books. Just speaking with Tuesday had her very confident that she would be the best to help her handle her business financials. They fell into a comfortable conversation about the business, while Tuesday began to take notes.

Sunni was captivated by Tuesday's perfect smile, laugh, and her wit. She didn't want her appointment to come to an end, but she knew that she couldn't stay here all day.

"You have given me much to think about," Sunni murmured, looking down at her own notes that she had been taking. Tuesday was a wealth of knowledge, sharing things with her that her old accountant hadn't informed her of. She stood and began gathering all of her paperwork that they had spread out on Tuesday's desk. "Should I make another appointment with you soon?"

"I would say, let's meet back in a month," Tuesday replied, helping gather the papers. Their hands bumped into each other as they reached for the same folder. Sunni's eyes flew to Tuesday's, and time seemed to stand still. Staring into Tuesday's green eyes this close, she could see the flecks of gold that were scattered in her irises. The air was ripped from her lungs as she watched Tuesday's eyes drop to her lips.

Unconsciously, she ran her tongue along her bottom lip, as it suddenly felt dry.

"I hope you don't think I'm being too bold in asking, but would you like to go out tonight with me?" Sunni watched as her skin flushed the most beautiful shade of red as she tucked her hair behind her ear. "I've only been here a few weeks and I was invited by Lyric to come out with her mate and another couple. I'd love to have you as my date."

Sunni stared at Tuesday as she rambled on. Little did the accountant know she had her at 'go out.' Sunni wouldn't care if the date was to hear tax law lectures, she'd be there in a heartbeat.

"I would love to," she breathed, turning toward Tuesday, papers forgotten. She could no longer resist. She just had to know what her lips tasted like.

She reached for Tuesday, grabbing her by the nape of her neck and crushed her lips to hers. Tuesday's mouth instantly opened and greeted Sunni's tongue with hers.

Sunni's wolf let loose a howl.

This was their mate.

CHAPTER THREE

Tuesday ran her comb through her hair one last time and noticed how her hand trembled. She willed her nerves to calm down. She couldn't show up for her date a basket case. The kiss she shared with Sunni earlier in her office left one hell of an impression on her. It had taken her the whole time that they had worked through Sunni's business numbers for her to gather up the nerve to ask Sunni out.

Sealing the offer with a kiss had been a bonus. The minute Sunni's lips touched hers, her wolf began clawing at her chest, demanding to be let out. It had taken everything she had to not lay Sunni out on her desk and have her wicked way with her.

Her wolf disagreed. She had frantically clawed at Tuesday's insides so that she could break free.

To greet their mate.

It had been confirmed.

Sunni Vinson was her mate.

That kiss was the kiss of all kisses. Never before had she experience such an explosion of emotions by a simple kiss.

But it wasn't *just* a kiss.

It was the first kiss she'd shared with her mate.

Tonight, Lyric had set up for them to go out to a bar for food and drinks, and then a run. She was itching to let her wolf out so that she could get to know her new territory. Her home wasn't far from her office, and had a nice back yard that ran into a small wooded area.

Moon Valley was a great area that was close to nature, and was the perfect town for shifters who would need a lot of room to roam.

The sound of her cell phone ringing broke through her thoughts. She glanced at herself one last time before rushing out of her en suite bathroom and grabbed her phone from her nightstand.

She smiled, seeing that it was her mom. She swiped the glass screen and answered. It had been a few days since she'd last spoken with her mother. She had much to catch her up on.

"Hey, Mom," she breathed, sitting on the edge of her bed. She would need to pick Sunni up in twenty minutes, and would briefly take her mother's call to check in.

"Well hello, dear," Sharon Webb greeted her. The sound of her mother's voice made her a little homesick, but she pushed it down. Moon Valley was to be her home now. She could always go and visit her mother any time she wanted. "Are you all settled into your new place?"

"Yes, I am. How is everyone?" She was sure her mother would have juicy information on everyone from the neighborhood that she grew up in. Her mother was sort of the town gossip.

If there was information needed, Sharon probably had it.

"The family is doing fine. Your brother is itching to come visit you, but I think I've persuaded him to wait a little bit. I swear that boy acts like you've moved to the other end of the Earth."

She chuckled, knowing that her brother probably wouldn't be listening to their mother. Tod was extremely protective of her, and she expected he'd be stopping by any day now. She was actually surprised he hadn't came by yet. She was only an hour away from home and was easily accessible from her hometown.

"Well thanks, Mom. I'll be inviting you all down soon. I just need to put some final touches on my house and the office, and an invitation will be in the mail. You're going to love my house."

"Take your time, dear. I'm confident you're going to do well in your new home and town. Moon Valley was a good decision. It's a good town, and the alpha is a strong one. I know you're in good hands with Kortan's pack. So, anything good happening tonight for you?" She could hear the real question in her mom's vague tone.

"Well, I've met someone, Mom," she whispered. She laughed as her mother squealed into the phone. Sharon Webb was trying her best to get both of her children mated off. Tuesday's father, Roland Webb, had been killed in a tragic accident over ten years ago, and it was just the three of them left. Sharon desperately wanted grandpups of her own to start spoiling since she was officially living alone.

"Already?" her mother gushed. She could imagine her mother rushing to her favorite recliner and taking a seat so she could hear the latest gossip. "You've only been there a couple of weeks."

"I know. It was just a chance meeting."

"And who is this someone?" her mother asked.

A vision of Sunni came to Tuesday's mind. A curvy brunette with fire in her eyes and a mouth of a goddess. Tuesday's lips still tingled with the memory of their kiss. Not that she was hoping for much action on their first date, but she sure hoped they'd have a repeat kiss tonight.

"Her name is Sunni and she owns the town's coffee shop," she announced. She held her breath, unsure of how her Mom would really react to the announcement.

"Honey, I may not be near you, but I can sense that you're worried about what I would think." Sharon laughed. "As long as the person makes you smile, takes care of you and loves you unconditionally, that's all that matters." Tuesday sighed, feeling relieved. It wasn't that she hadn't been open with her mother before. She'd dated both males and females in the past, but this time, she knew that Sunni was the one.

Her only concern was that she didn't know how her mother would act about her settling down with a female.

"I think—no, I know, she's my mate," Tuesday announced, waiting to see how her mother would respond.

"Really? Well, I am really intrigued. You hurry and get that invitation in the mail so I can have an excuse to come down there to Moon Valley and see who has stolen my daughter's heart."

"Yes, ma'am."

CHAPTER FOUR

Tuesday pulled her small, older sedan up to the apartment building that Sunni lived in. Her compact car had seen better days, but it was still running perfectly. She smiled, thinking of how well her business was taking off, and that soon, she'd upgrade and get a bigger one. At the moment, it was just her so she didn't really need a larger vehicle, and it still purred like a dream.

She glanced at the building, double checking that she had the correct address. It was located in what was considered downtown Moon Valley, two blocks from the Little Bean Coffee Shop. The building wasn't a large apartment building. The brick structure stood about three stories tall and looked like a nice place to live. She parked on the curb, but before she could turn the car off, Sunni came bounding out of the front door with a wide smile on her face.

"Hey, you." Sunni smiled as she climbed into the car, slamming the door shut behind her.

"Hey—" Her words were cut off by Sunni's mouth. She gasped as Sunni's tongue thrust between her lips. Her body automatically responded to her mate's. She groaned as Sunni entwined her fingers in her hair, anchoring them together as she thoroughly kissed her. Their lips moved in perfect rhythm.

She'd never experienced a kiss that literally took her breath away. At the moment, Sunni's kiss was consuming her, and she didn't have any complaint as their tongues stroked each other's.

Moisture collected at the apex of her thighs, soaking her panties. She wanted this wolf and apparently, Sunni wanted her too. The smell of Sunni's arousal filled the small car. She released a protest as Sunni pulled back and placed a chaste kiss to her lips. She opened her eyes and found Sunni gazing into her eyes, with a smile playing on her lips.

"Well, hello to you too," she murmured, reaching up to stroke Sunni's cheek. She'd had half a mind to text Lyric that she wasn't coming so that her and Sunni could finish what they had started.

Hell, Tuesday didn't care if they finished it right here in her car for anyone to see. The kiss had her strung so tight that her clit ached to have this little wolf's tongue on it.

"I've been wanting to do that ever since I left you this morning," Sunni admitted, settling back in her seat. Tuesday's eyes roamed her mate's body and bit back a curse. Sunni was a sexy woman and she knew it. She was dressed in a short mini skirt, a halter top that left her back open, and heeled sandals.

"Well, I'm glad you got it out of your system," she giggled, putting the car into drive and pulling away from the curb. From the directions on her phone, it would take them about twenty minutes to reach the bar. It was located away from downtown and deep in the woods to allow people to shift and enjoy the woods.

Her eyes were drawn to the smooth span of skin that was on display. Her fingers itched to discover if the skin on Sunni's legs were as smooth as they appeared.

Down girl, she chanted in her head. *No groping her on the first date.*

"Not by a long shot," Sunni murmured, causing Tuesday's eyes to flash to her. In the dark car, Tuesday could see the sensual smile spread across Sunni's face.

Her heart slammed against her chest as Sunni's hand took her free one. She entwined their fingers together, leaving Tuesday to drive with one hand. She glanced over and cast a smile to Sunni, pleased that she was feeling what Tuesday was.

"How was your day?" she asked, trying to make idle conversation. There wasn't much traffic out at this time of night in Moon Valley, so their ride shouldn't take too long. She had to beat down her beast that kept pushing forward. Her animal wanted to connect with Sunni's, but now was not the time. They'd have time for that later when they all went for their run after dinner and drinks.

"Long," Sunni replied with a chuckle. "I had the pleasure of tasting the most sweetest lips this morning, being invited out on a date with the owner of said lips, and then being left all day to fantasize about the owner."

"How dare she!" Tuesday exclaimed, her lips tilted up in a small smile.

"I know. She was such as tease."

Tuesday's breath caught in her throat as she felt Sunni tug her hand toward her lap as she braked at a red stop light.

"And what did you fantasize about?" she whispered, liking where this game was going. Sunni slid their hands beneath her skirt and guided Tuesday's hand to her pantyless pussy. Her eyes flew to Sunni's hooded ones as she parted her legs.

"These fingers being coated in my juices? My pussy has been soaked ever since leaving your office. I wanted to show you how much you've affected me."

Sunni gasped as Tuesday parted her labia, finding her swollen clit. She didn't need any further instructions. Exploring Sunni's soaked pussy would make this ride very interesting. She glanced around and noticed that they were alone on the road and the light was still red.

"This is all for me?" she asked, stroking the bundle of nerves, eliciting a deep moan from Sunni. The woman wasn't kidding either. Her pussy was soaked, making Tuesday wish she could lap up the juices with her tongue. She loved how wide Sunni had herself open, allowing her fingers to explore her soaked pussy folds. She glanced down and noticed that somehow, Sunni's skirt was now bunched up on her hips, leaving her bare for Tuesday to see and touch everything. "Recline your seat back more," she suggested, wanting to take advantage of Sunni offering herself to her.

Sunni immediately followed her orders, laying her seat back halfway. In her new position, it allowed Tuesday to have more access to her delicious smelling pussy. There was no way that they were stopping this little game.

The smell of Sunni's arousal reached Tuesday's nostrils. She breathed in deeply, fighting her fangs from descending.

She cursed. Not only were they in the compact car, but in the middle of an intersection.

"Yes," Sunni hissed, her head thrown back against

the headrest of her seat as Tuesday stroked her clitoris. Her fingers moved on their own accord, sliding deep within Sunni's soaked folds before encircling her clitoris again. She stroked the little bundle of nerves, causing Sunni to thrust her hips against her hand.

The light turned green and there was no way that Tuesday was removing her fingers. She'd be driving the rest of the way with one hand. Putting her foot on the gas, she continued on with her left hand guiding the car. The highway remained empty as she drove. As they moved farther away from the intersection, they became surrounded by darkness.

Moisture seeped from her own pussy as she continued to finger Sunni. As much as her body was begging for a release, she'd have to wait. Her fingers were drenched from Sunni's arousal and she was tempted to pull her car over to the side of the road so they could hop in the back seat and finish each other off.

"Oh, God. Don't stop," Sunni cried out, thrusting her pelvis forward. She braced her arms against the seats as she arched her back and her hips. The air in the car was thick with their arousal. Anyone with a nose, not even a shifter's, would be able to smell it in the air.

"You couldn't make me if you tried," she muttered as her fingers frantically worked Sunni's clitoris. She slid her fingers farther into her mate's pussy, gathering more of her moisture and dragging it to the small bundle of nerves. She used her hand to massage and grip Sunni's mound. "What I wouldn't give to have this pussy on my mouth right now."

Driving with her fingers deep inside of Sunni took great concentration. If ever before she needed the skills of multitasking, now would be the time. Thank goodness, she was a master at doing more than one thing at a time. Her mate must have needed a release, and she knew deep in her heart that she'd do anything for Sunni.

And if giving her release on the highway was what she wanted, then a release on the highway she would get.

Her fingers, having a mind of their own, slid along Sunni's entire pussy, coating all five fingers in Sunni's arousal. Sunni's cries of ecstasy filled the air, eliciting a growl from Tuesday. Her wolf paced inside of her chest, sensing their mate. She dipped her fingers as deep as they could go inside of Sunni's core. Her eyes glanced over at Sunni and found her to be the most beautiful sight.

She was naked from the waist down with her legs wide, showcasing her pussy just for Tuesday.

Perfection.

"Pull your breasts out so I can see them," she

growled, flicking Sunni's clit fast and hard. The only thing that was missing was the sight of Sunni's plump mounds. Sunni immediately released the clasp at the back of her neck, freeing her bountiful breasts. She didn't need any further instructions and began pinching and tugging on her own nipples.

Tuesday bit her lip to keep from cursing. Her tongue begged to bathe Sunni's nipples.

"Tuesday, I need your mouth on me," Sunni groaned, her head thrown back.

"Baby, I wish I could right now," she murmured, her eyes flickering back and forth from the road to Sunni's naked mounds. Her fingers moved in fast strokes, jerking the little bundle of nerves. Sunni thrust her core against Tuesday's hand, begging for more. "So you've been thinking of me all day, huh?"

Her animal was close to the surface. She had to fight to keep her incisors from descending. Her beast wanted to sink her fangs deep into Sunni, marking her forever in the way of shifters.

"Yes. Oh my—" Sunni's words turned incomprehensible as her body writhed in her seat as Tuesday applied more pressure to her clit. She pinched Sunni's clit, eliciting a scream as her muscles tightened. Sunni's legs clamped down, trapping Tuesday's hand as her body shook. She chanted Tuesday's name as she coasted through her release.

Tuesday's eyes flickered back and forth between Sunni and the road as she guided them along the dark highway. She smiled as Sunni's body relaxed in the chair. If she didn't know any better, Sunni had fallen into a hard sleep just that quick. She pulled her drenched fingers from her lover's pussy and brought them to her lips with a smile.

CHAPTER FIVE

Sunni had a hard time keeping her hands to herself as they sat in the large circle booth with the other couples. If she wasn't holding Tuesday's hand, she was rubbing her hand on Tuesday's bare leg, or wrapping her arm around her. She just needed to touch her.

Lyric and Libby, Sage and Meadow, apparently had the same problem. Each couple was sitting close to each other, always touching each other in some way. Their food had been delicious, and now they just sat back laughing and talking, as if they all had been friends for years.

The atmosphere in the bar was that of blaring country music, couples dancing on the dance floor, and lots of laughs. It was a typical small town bar and Sunni was truly enjoying herself.

Sunni knew the other couples from belonging to the same pack. She wasn't close friends with them, but would speak whenever she ran into them around town. After tonight, she had a feeling that they would all be longtime friends.

"So you two just met?" Libby, the alpha's sister, asked. Not only was Libby the alpha's sister, but she was one of the most famous shifter models in the world. Her mate and assistant, Lyric, smiled with a wistful look on her face as she turned to Libby.

"Yes, we did. Just a few days ago," Tuesday replied, turning to Sunni with a smile.

Sunni pulled Tuesday to her, keeping her arm around her. Their drive to the bar had been amazing. She had been painfully aroused all day just thinking of Tuesday. She knew the minute she got in the car that she wouldn't be able to control herself. She should be embarrassed about falling into a brief slumber, but she wasn't. Her orgasm was so powerful, is sucked the energy right out of her and put her fast asleep.

"I think that's so sweet. It's almost like looking at ourselves in the mirror." Meadow laughed. She was the local kindergarten teacher, and her mate, Sage, was the only female enforcer of the pack. Sunni had always been impressed by the enforcer. It was good to see that their alpha was open to female protectors. "Tuesday, Lyric and I are all new to the town.

Maybe it's something about Moon Valley and its residents."

They all shared a chuckle as they looked at each other. Maybe it was Moon Valley. Sunni smiled as she gazed into Tuesday's eyes. She could still smell her arousal on Tuesday's hands and lips. She had awakened in the car to Tuesday cleaning her fingers. The sight had immediately turned her on again.

"So how did you all meet?" Tuesday asked the other couples. Sunni was trying to pay attention to the conversation, but was having a hard time concentrating on anything else. The activities in Tuesday's car was replaying over and over in her head. Her core clenched with the thought of her mate's fingers in between her folds again. They had zipped from zero to a hundred fast, and Sunni didn't regret one second of their little tryst in the car.

Hell, she wanted to do it again.

It was so hot to be finger fucked in a car, in public, where anyone could see.

She bit her lip, knowing that she had to be careful. They were sitting at a table with other wolf shifters, and they would all be able to scent her arousal. Her eyes took in Tuesday, and she knew being caught would be totally worth it. Her eyes traveled down to Tuesday's magical hands and the memory of her fingers working her clit had her shifting in her seat.

She wanted more.

Tuesday, entranced in the wolves' stories, unconsciously reached out and grabbed Sunni's hand in hers.

She clenched her legs together.

It was going to be very difficult to not be aroused.

"Well, I was hired as an assistant to the alpha's sister. Little did I know she was *the* Liberty Glenn," Lyric chuckled, laying a kiss on Libby's cheek.

"She was the best assistant a girl could ask for," Libby chimed in. Sunni could hear Tuesday sigh at the romantic tale. Tuesday leaned into Sunni and ran her hand along her bare thigh, before settling it at the edge of her skirt. She bit her lip to keep from opening her legs for her mate's hand to travel higher.

Just a few inches higher and Tuesday's fingers could part her labia.

"As for us, I was the new school teacher trying to break up two little pups from fighting. They had shifted, both for the first time—" Meadow's words were cut off by her mate.

"And little Miss School Teacher in the killer heels thought she'd break them up. She got knocked down and I had to come to the rescue." Sage laughed, shaking her head.

"I had it handled," Meadow scoffed, gently slapping Sage's shoulder with the back of her hand.

"Sure you did. You were off work for about a week recovering," Sage taunted.

"And as I recall, you were there to comfort me and keep me very entertained." Meadow smiled at Sage, who planted a small kiss to her lips.

"Both of your stories are so encouraging. Thanks for sharing," Tuesday murmured, her eyes flickering to Sunni. She already knew their story, and hopefully, their ending would be like the other couples.

Mated.

"So, are you ladies up for a friendly run?" Sage asked with a cocked eyebrow.

"Yes! I need to stretch out my legs," Tuesday groaned. "I've been waiting to be able to explore more of Moon Valley in my wolf form."

"It would be best that your wolf get to know the territory." Sage nodded, the enforcer in her always at the forefront. "These lands out here are property of the pack, so it will be safe."

"Well, let's go let our wolves out," Sunni chirped, standing from the booth. She reached out a hand for Tuesday, helping her up. She entwined their fingers together, not wanting to break contact from Tuesday. Her wolf was pacing, ready to meet her mate.

It was time.

CHAPTER SIX

Sunni felt her wolf grin as they ran through the woods. The two wolves nipped and played with each other as they ran. Her wolf guided Tuesday's along, not wanting to put too much distance between them. Tuesday's wolf was a magnificent light brown wolf. She fell behind Sunni in a trot as they roamed the woods. They had separated from the other two couples about a half hour ago, wanting some privacy.

Sunni loved how well her and Tuesday's wolves were behaving.

Like mates.

They were deep in the woods, the sounds and smells of the wild surrounding them. She had lost track of time, and how long they had been in the woods. It wouldn't matter since Tuesday had driven her car. They wouldn't need to meet up with the other couples. Before shifting, they had agreed to go out again soon, knowing that once in the woods, there was no telling how long they'd be out there.

Sunni came to a small cozy opening in the woods and paused. The lush grass and brushes were beautiful, and she wanted to share the beauty of nature with her mate.

In their human form.

She pulled back on her animal, ordering herself to change. Her body began the shift, with her bones and body switching back to her human form. Within minutes, her body was that of a naked human again.

She stood from her kneeling position and watched as Tuesday shifted.

"It's so beautiful out here," Tuesday gushed, turning around in a circle.

"It is," she replied, unable to take her eyes off Tuesday's lush, naked curves. Her full breasts were perky, with pink areolas. Her waist was tapered in with her hips flaring out, highlighting her round ass.

Sunni's feet moved on their own as she pushed Tuesday up against a tree. She covered Tuesday's mouth with hers before she could say another word. Sunni pressed her body against her mate's, loving the feeling of their breasts brushing against each other. They both groaned, rubbing their bodies together. Tuesday's soft skin drove Sunni crazy. She made a note to taste every inch of it tonight.

She thrust her tongue past Tuesday's lips. Their kiss was hot, open, and wet. Tuesday's hands roamed her body, driving her crazy as they made their way to Sunni's ass. She groaned as Tuesday gripped and cupped her ass cheeks. She tore her lips from Tuesday's and trailed her tongue along her jawline and down her neck, getting a taste of her mate. The slight hint of saltiness coated her skin and drove her wolf wild.

Her gums burned as her incisors threatened to break through. She fought hard to keep them from descending because if they did, it would be very hard to keep from marking Tuesday with a mating bite.

"Yes," Tuesday hissed as Sunni cupped her large mounds, bringing the first to her mouth. She enclosed her mouth around Tuesday's beaded nipple, sucking as much of it into her mouth as she could. She closed her eyes as she focused on suckling her mate's breasts. She took her time, pulling back on the nipple before sucking it back farther into her mouth.

Her hand, full with one plump mound, massaged the other as she focused on the first. Her hands weren't large enough to completely cover Tuesday's breasts. Sunni loved the feel of Tuesdays' soft beaded nipple as she pinched it, eliciting a gasp from Tuesday. She smiled against her mate's soft flesh, loving the response. Tuesday's fingers threaded their way in her hair, holding her anchored to her breasts. Sunni tore her mouth from the first and blazed a trail with her tongue as she moved over to the second one, kneeling on the ground before her mate.

Tonight, they had all the time in the world. She wanted to take her time in exploring her woman's supple body.

She nipped the beaded nipple before soothing it with her tongue, then blazed a hot trail down Tuesday's abdomen.

"I know I told you earlier that I fantasized about your fingers in my pussy," she murmured against the soft skin of Tuesday's belly. She trailed her hands up to massage Tuesday's breasts as she bathed her navel with her tongue. She wanted to taste every part of Tuesday and would do so tonight. They were in their own little corner of the world, and her wolf could sense that they were the only two people in the area. "But this was truly what I was fantasizing about."

She pushed Tuesday's legs apart and enclosed her mouth on her mate's pussy. She used her tongue to lick up all the moisture that had gathered in between her folds. The tanginess exploded on her tongue as she sucked and licked every part she could reach.

"Sunni, yes," Tuesday groaned, spreading her legs farther as she braced against the tree. Her fingers clenched in Sunni's hair, holding her in place. Sunni loved being on her knees in front of her mate. She grabbed one of Tuesday's legs and pulled it over her shoulder to open Tuesday's center to her. Pleasuring Tuesday was her mission, and she took this job very seriously.

She continued to pay close attention to Tuesday's clit while sliding a finger deep inside of Tuesday core. Her fingers became drenched in her lover's arousal. The tight channel stretched as she thrust her fingers in and out.

"You taste as good as I knew you would," she groaned, feeling her own arousal slide from in between her legs. She continued thrusting her finger deep inside of Tuesday, adding a second one. Her eyes were mesmerized by the sight of Tuesday's juices coating her fingers. She thrust them deep, leaning forward to suckle Tuesday's swollen clitoris. The swollen bundle of nerves called to her. She nipped and licked the flesh, drawing a deep moan from Tuesday. She was already addicted to the tanginess of Tuesday's pussy.

She wanted more.

"Let me sit on your face," Tuesday murmured, pulling Sunni's head away from her core.

A woman after her own heart.

Sunni immediately pulled back, smiling as they moved together. She laid down on the soft grass with Tuesday covering her body with hers, took her mouth, kissing her deeply. She took advantage of her lover's body on hers, gripping Tuesday's ass tightly in her hands.

"How about you flip around and we taste each other?" she suggested against Tuesday's lips. She could see the flash of heat in her mate's eyes in the moonlight as she nodded her head. Tuesday shifted her body, placing her pussy directly over Sunni's face.

She growled at being able to have her mate's entire core at her disposal. She eagerly spread her own legs as she felt the hot breath of her mate's face in between her legs.

Gripping Tuesday's ass cheeks in her hands, she pulled her soaked pussy to her mouth, swiping Tuesday's entire pussy with her tongue. She used the wide girth of her tongue to taste every facet of Tuesday's pussy. Her nose was buried deep in Tuesdays folds, exploring it. She wasn't going to last long.

She frantically consumed all of Tuesday as her mate returned the favor. The sounds of licking and sucking filled the air as they both devoured each other. She spread Tuesday's labia far apart as she latched onto the swollen clitoris, sucking hard to draw more of it into her mouth. She pulled back on it, stretching it and letting go. She repeated the motion, as Tuesday ground her pussy into Sunni's mouth.

Sunni's breaths were coming fast, as Tuesday was a demanding lover. She had latched onto Sunni's clit and shook her head while humming. Sunni thrust her pussy farther into her lover's greedy mouth. She could feel the sensation of her orgasm building. Sunni gripped Tuesday tight as she latched onto her clit, this time not letting go. To enhance the feeling for her mate, she gathered some of Tuesday's arousal and coated her anus. She gently slid a single digit deep within her puckered anus as she continued to suck on Tuesday's swollen clitoris. Tuesday cried out at the new invasion, tipping her over into her orgasm.

They both crested at the same time, their orgasms slamming into them simultaneously.

Their cries filled the air as they both switched to using their fingers to ensure the other one reached their full peak.

"Oh, my. Sunni," Tuesday gasped, her breaths coming fast.

"Tuesday..." Sunni didn't know what to say. Did she call her mate? There no way that Tuesday didn't feel it. Their wolves belonged together. Instead of saying something that could potentially ruin the night, she took it upon herself to use her tongue to clean all the evidence of her mate's release.

They had plenty of time to figure this out.

CHAPTER SEVEN

Tuesday's wolf was almost fully satisfied. What would have made her wolf feel fulfilled would be fully mating with Sunni. She smiled as she lounged on top of her mate. She loved the feel of Sunni's soft skin against hers. Tuesday wasn't sure why, but she'd always been more attracted to females than males. It was something about a woman's body that just drew her in. Sunni's body was amazing. Her breasts, her hips, pussy and ass just drove Tuesday crazy.

There wasn't a part of her woman's body that she hadn't tasted or loved. She smiled, just feeling happy. They had made it back to Sunni's apartment and spent practically all weekend in bed.

"I don't want to go back to reality." Sunni pouted as

she slowly caressed Tuesday's back. It was as if she had read Tuesday's mind.

Tomorrow, she would have to go back to the office. She had an interview with a potential secretary, and Sunni had to report back to her business. The past forty-eight hours, they had taken the time to get to know each other. Not only did they explore each other's bodies, but got to know all about each other as well.

They shared everything from their childhood to their hopes and dreams of the future.

They both tiptoed gently around the elephant in the room.

Mating.

"Me either," she murmured, running her hand along Sunni's cheek. She loved how soft her lover's skin was. It tasted as good as it smelled too. She trailed her fingers down her sternum to her beaded nipples. "I love the taste of you."

She shifted down slightly so that she could suckle on Sunni's full breasts.

The slight intake of Sunni's breath urged her on. She knew that Sunni loved her suckling her breasts. Sunni cradled her to her chest as she bathed her nipple with her tongue. Tuesday held the breast steady to allow her to gently lick the beaded nipple that was standing at attention. She sucked the tit deep within her mouth, filling it to capacity.

"I wish I could take you to work with me," Sunni murmured. Her breasts jiggled with her giggles. Tuesday smiled against the tempting breast as she shifted to the side to allow her fingers to move along Sunni's body. She switched breasts, not wanting the other one to feel abandoned.

"Really? And what would you want me there for?" She would play along with the fantasy. She was interested in hearing what Sunni had dreamt up. All weekend, they'd had fun with role playing and toys. There hadn't been one boring moment, and Tuesday was interested in hearing the latest fantasy of her lover.

Her fingers trailed down farther toward Sunni's core. She dipped her fingers in between Sunni's slick folds, stroking her swollen clit as she rotated her nipple with her tongue. Sunni's legs parted to allow Tuesday's fingers to continue dancing along her bundle of nerves. She bit back a growl, loving how her mate's body responded to her.

"Oh, let's see. You would be in my office, working on my books. The shop would be fully staffed at the counter and wouldn't need me. I'd decide to go back to the office to work on payroll or something, and that's where I would find you working. I'd shut the door so that the noise from the shop wouldn't bother our concentration."

"Yes, because I'm so easy to distract," Tuesday joked, lazily stroking Sunni's clit. She loved the sound of Sunni's fantasy so far, and wanted her to continue sharing. Tuesday continued sensually sucking on Sunni's taut nipples.

"Yes, I know. That's why I would leave you be and sit at my desk to work on my computer. You would become so distracted by me that you would crawl toward me on your knees and disappear beneath my desk without me even knowing it, until you parted my legs." Sunni moaned slightly as Tuesday slid a finger deep within her core. She pulled back and introduced a second one, slowly thrusting them deep. Sunni rotated her hips, syncing with the motion of Tuesday's fingers. She pulled back and introduced a third, stretching her mate to capacity. Her thumb slowly massaged her clit as she filled Sunni with her fingers.

"Keep going," Tuesday murmured, urging her on. She needed to hear the rest of the story while she sensually tortured Sunni. She nipped her lover's nipple with her incisors that had descended. No use in fighting them today. It was the animal in her. She quickly soothed the beaded nipple as she swirled it around with her tongue. She sucked as much of the mound in her mouth as she could, again filling her mouth to capacity with a soft breast.

"I'll be wearing a skirt and no panties. You'll spread my legs wide. Your tongue will go deep in my pussy and it will be so fucking sexy seeing you eat my pussy while in my office, and making me have one hell of an orgasm. But I'll have to be quiet because we wouldn't want my employees to know that my accountant was currently getting me off."

"Sounds delicious," Tuesday commented, pulling her fingers from Sunni's pussy and bringing them to her mouth to clean them. She couldn't get enough of Sunni's pussy juices. They were sweet and tangy all at the same time, and she was addicted.

She dipped her fingers into Sunni's pussy again, gathering more of her arousal, but this time, she offered her fingers to Sunni, who didn't hesitate in opening her mouth. She let loose a growl as she watched Sunni grip her wrist to suck and lick each finger clean.

"You are so fucking sexy," she growled, repeating her motion to collect more of Sunni's juices. This time, she was greedy and kept them for herself.

"You love it too," Sunni quipped, sitting up in the bed with a glint in her eyes. The look held a promise of pleasure coming Tuesday's way. Sunni's wolf was the more dominate of the two, and Tuesday loved having their lovemaking controlled by her mate. She always benefited from it. "Let's play."

Tuesday chuckled as she watched her mate bound from the bed and walk over to her closet, where she disappeared for a brief moment. Since arriving Friday night, she had learned that her mate had quite a stash of toys and loved to use them on Tuesday and herself.

"What do you have in mind?" she asked, her breaths coming fast as she watched Sunni come out of the closet with a large strap-on strapped to her body. The fake cock was long and wide. Her heart jumped as she sat up on the bed, her eyes locked on the large cock. Her pussy pulsed, ready to feel it deep within her. Her mate knew what she liked, and knew that Tuesday loved her taking her every way possible. She licked her lips as she crawled over to the edge of the bed, ready to play any game her mate wanted to play.

"Come here, Tuesday." She stood from the bed and took a few steps toward Sunni. She knelt before her, wanting to take her cock deep in her throat. "Suck my cock, baby."

"Yes, ma'am." Tuesday smiled up at Sunni as she gripped the wide cock in her hand.

Her core clenched with the thought of taking it deep inside of her. Her eyes locked with Sunni's as she licked the full length, before swallowing as much as she could. Sunni threaded her fingers in her hair as she pulled back. She gripped the base of it before sucking it deep in her mouth again. She couldn't wait to see what it would feel like inside of her.

"You're such a dirty girl," Sunni murmured, guiding it into Tuesday's mouth. Tuesday was strung tight, loving everything about Sunni, who was very adventurous in the bedroom. "You suck cock like a pro."

"For you, anything," she admitted, stroking the cock in her hand. Sunni's eyebrows jerked up. Her breath caught in her throat, as she could see the wheels turning in her mate's head.

"Really?" Sunni asked, trailing a finger along Tuesday's bottom lip. "I'll have to keep that in mind. Now come here, dirty girl."

Tuesday giggled as Sunni helped her from the floor and guided her back to the bed. Sunni pushed her down onto her stomach as she came up behind her. Tuesday didn't need any instructions, she eagerly got on all fours, putting her ass on display for Sunni.

"This ass is just absolutely perfect," Sunni murmured, slapping Tuesday on her right cheek. She groaned and shook her ass, wanting Sunni to do it again. Her core clenched in anticipation of feeling the thick cock fill her.

"Sunni, please," she gasped. Sunni teased her, sliding the tip along her pussy. She braced herself, spreading her legs wide. She could feel her arousal drip from her as the cock brushed her labia.

"Please what?"

"Fuck me," she practically screamed as Sunni slammed the cock deep inside of her. Her pussy burned slightly as her walls stretched to accommodate the girth. Sunni pulled back, only leaving the tip before she repeated the motion. Tuesday cried out, loving the force and the feeling of her pussy being stretched so wide. They would need to use this toy often. "Yes! Fuck me harder."

Her fingers dug into the blankets as she thrust her hips back, taking the cock deep inside of her pussy. Sunni's fingers dug into her hips with every thrust. Her body began to shake as Sunni pounded the cock deep. Her pussy walls gripped it tight as Sunni continued. Being a shifter, she could take rough sex. Shifters healed much quicker than humans. Any marks, cuts, and bruises would be healed within hours.

They got into a good rhythm as Tuesday rocked back and forth, meeting every one of Sunni's hard thrusts. The sounds of skin slapping and cries of ecstasy filled the air. It was the most arousing sound she'd ever heard.

"Play with your clit, Tuesday," Sunni commanded. She immediately followed her instructions, balancing herself to allow her to slide her hand to her pussy. Her finger had blazed this trail a million times and knew the way to her clit. She coated her fingers in her juices before settling on her swollen flesh. She began to frantically rub herself while Sunni continued her rhythm with the strap on.

Her muscles began to tighten and clenched down on the cock as she grew closer to release. She had lost count of the amount of orgasms Sunni had dragged from her, and this was going to be a hard one, the best kind.

She cried out as the waves of her orgasm washed over her. Her body jerked as she continued to flick her clit. Sunni stilled her movements as Tuesday gasped and shook from the power of her orgasm. She dropped down on her elbows, trying to catch her breath. The cock was still buried deep inside her, giving her a delicious full feeling that she loved.

"I'm not done with you yet, Tuesday," Sunni chuckled, withdrawing the cock. Her core pulsed as if demanding the cock return. "Come clean me off."

A grin spread across Tuesday's face as she pushed off the bed. She turned around and took in Sunni kneeling on the bed, with her cock glistening in Tuesday's juices. Tuesday licked her lips, loving how Sunni was taking control of their relationship. She had no complaints of being the submissive wolf in the relationship.

Not at all.

It was the way of their kind.

"Yes, ma'am," she murmured, crawling to Sunni. She gripped the slick cock and did as she was instructed.

CHAPTER EIGHT

Tuesday and Sunni had settled into a routine, taking turns on where they would sleep. Some nights they would sleep over Tuesday's house, and some nights, Sunni's apartment. Weeks had flown by, and Sunni was still floating on cloud nine. Tuesday was everything that she could ever want in a woman. The sex between them was out of this world. Sunni's appetite for Tuesday was voracious. She couldn't get enough of her lover.

Soon, she'd bring up the word they were both avoiding.

Mating.

They'd gone out a couple times with the girls, and were now officially considered a couple. She tried to push Tuesday from her mind, but she knew that it would be useless. Her mate had ingrained herself into her very being.

"Anything else we need out the back?" she asked Laura, one of her employees. She was doing some stocking while the crew was handling the lunch crowd.

"No, we're good. I think we can handle it, boss. Don't you have something to do in your office?" Laura cocked an eyebrow at her.

Sunni hated paperwork, but knew Laura was hinting at said paperwork.

"Well, if you think you guys are okay..." She looked around, trying to find something else to do. "Do the tables need to be wiped down?"

"Nope. Mike will handle that." Laura shook her head. "You have me and Cindy here today. I'm serious, we're good. Go." Laura laughed as she pointed toward the back of the shop.

"Okay," she groaned, rolling her eyes. Having her two lead baristas should have meant she could be housed up in her office, but she didn't want to tackle the mound of work that was piling up on her desk.

Maybe it would magically take care of itself.

"Morning," a familiar voice called out. Sunni turned to find Tuesday walking into the shop, carrying her messenger bag.

"Hey, honey. What are you doing here?" she asked, glad to see her. It was ironic how she had been trying to get Tuesday out of her mind, and then here she went, showing up.

"I told you that we should meet in about a month so that we can keep your books up." Tuesday waved and smiled at the crew.

Sunni hadn't mentioned to her staff that she was dating Tuesday, wanting to keep her personal life separate from work. Not that she was hiding Tuesday, she just wanted to stay professional. If someone asked, then she would gladly admit it, but for now, her staff only knew that Tuesday was going to be keeping the books for the shop.

"Okay. Well, head in the back. Apparently my staff is kicking me out. I'll join you in a second."

Tuesday nodded and disappeared toward Sunni's office. She turned and found Laura's eyes on her. Her lead barista crossed her arms in front of her chest, her eyes threatening bodily harm.

"I'm just going to put this stuff up, and then I'll be out of your hair," she grumbled, holding her hands up in the air. At times, she couldn't tell if she was the boss or her employees were. She quickly finished stocking the counter. She had to admit, she had the best staff. The shop could practically run itself.

She took her apron off and walked toward the back. She had worn a dress today because her and Tuesday were supposed to be going out to dinner after work.

She smiled as she made her way to her office, finding Tuesday with her nose buried in her papers at the table in the corner. She shut the door and walked toward her desk.

"So they finally kicked you away from the counter, huh?" Tuesday chuckled, looking up from Sunni's cost reports.

"Yup. I guess they would want me to work on payroll. That seems to be important to them." She laughed, taking a seat at her desk. She typed in a few commands on her computer, pulling up the program she would need to work in. "So where are we going to dinner?"

She glanced up and didn't see Tuesday. She gasped as two hands parted her legs. She looked down and found Tuesday beneath her desk, sliding her dress up, and she grinned, knowing what Tuesday was doing.

Her fantasy.

"Well, I'm up for a snack right now," Tuesday murmured, a devilish look in her eyes as her hands slid up Sunni's thighs. "Our reservation isn't for another three hours."

"I might be able to help you with that." She cocked her eyebrow and spread her legs. She slid down in the chair to rest her ass on the edge of the seat to give Tuesday easy access to her.

"If I didn't know any better, I'd say you planned

this," Tuesday remarked. Her eyes flew to Sunni's once she realized that Sunni wasn't wearing any panties.

"I'm always ready for you," she responded. She hated panties, and right now, with her mate licking her pussy, it proved why she didn't need them. They would just be in the way. She gripped Tuesday's hair tight as she lost herself to the pleasure of her mate's tongue parting her slick folds.

Her animal rose to the surface, loving the sight of Tuesday on her knees with her face buried in her pussy. Tuesday's eyes locked with hers as she sucked on her clit. Sunni spread her legs wide, bringing her legs to rest on the armrests of her chair, her new position giving Tuesday full access to her.

"So good," Tuesday muttered, running her tongue along the full length of Sunni. "I can't get enough of you."

Sunni growled as she watched Tuesday thrust her tongue in her core. Tuesday kept her tongue erected, thrusting it forward, deep into Sunni's folds.

"Yes," she hissed. She couldn't take her eyes off Tuesday if someone held a gun to her head. The sight of her mate feasting on her was a big turn on. Tuesday's face was coated in her arousal. The sounds of slurping, licking, and growls filled the air. "Put those cute little fingers in my pussy, Tuesday."

Her animal was the more dominant between the

two, and she loved how Tuesday submitted to her. Tuesday didn't hesitate in sliding her two fingers deep within her core as she latched onto Sunni's clit.

Sunni gently brushed Tuesday's hair from her face, not wanting to miss one second of her mate's lips on her clit. Tuesday rotated from open mouth licking her pussy to suckling her clit.

"Make me come," she growled, holding Tuesday's face in place. She thrust her pussy against her mate's mouth as she latched on her clit. Tuesday sucked her clitoris deep, eliciting a deep grown from Sunni. At the moment, she couldn't keep quiet. She didn't care if her employees or customers heard her.

She was close to reaching her peak. She growled, riding Tuesday's face. Her mate's eyes were on her as she suckled her clit. She felt Tuesday's fingers withdraw from her core before trailing down to her puckered anus.

"Yes, do it," she groaned, giving her mate permission to invade her dark hole. She loved ass play, and right now, she was going to demand it. She cried out as Tuesday's fingers slid into her anus. She threw back her head and let loose a silent scream as she slammed into her releases. Her chest rose and fell hard as she basked in the feeling of euphoria. She slumped back in her chair as Tuesday gently continued to clean her pussy of release.

"How was that for fulfilling a fantasy?" Tuesday whispered.

"That was fucking amazing. I love you," she said, sitting forward. She pulled Tuesday to her and crushed her mouth to her mate's. Sunni could taste herself on Tuesday's tongue and loved it. The kiss grew more frantic.

She no longer wanted to dance around the mating word. She had been waiting for the perfect moment, and it was now.

She didn't care that they were in her office, in her place of business. If her employees walked in on them, they would catch an eyeful.

The kiss between them was hard, open, and full of passion and tongue.

"I love you too," Tuesday gasped, pulling back. Her eyes darkened as she gazed at Sunni.

"I've been wanting to say that for weeks now," Sunni admitted, pressing another kiss to Tuesday's lips.

"Me too," Tuesday confided, breaking their kiss again. Sunni's hands began to busy themselves. "What are you doing?"

"Taking off your clothes," Sunni murmured, nipping Tuesday's neck with her fangs. She removed Tuesday's dress and quickly undid her bra, freeing her bountiful breasts, then moved to rid Tuesday of her offending panties. "I'm about to take my mate on my desk."

"Your mate?" Tuesday paused Sunni's hands. Her eyes softened as she gazed into Sunni's eyes. She could see the love brimming from Tuesday's eyes at the mention of being mates. "You've felt it too?"

"Of course I did," Sunni admitted, standing from her chair. She placed Tuesday on her desk and gripped her face with her hands, softly brushing her lips against hers. "I've been waiting for the moment to ask, and I don't think that there will ever be a better time. Tuesday Webb, will you mate with me?"

Tuesday released a squeal and wrapped her arms around Sunni in a crushing hug.

"Yes." Tuesday laughed. Sunni leaned forward and kissed her mate. It turned desperate now that the air between them was cleared. Sunni wasn't sure why they both had tiptoed around the mating word, but now that it was out in the open, they could plan their future together.

She pinched her lover's nipples before pushing her back onto the desk, not caring that papers flew off onto the floor. Sunni let loose a small growl as she removed her own clothes so that they both were naked.

"Open up for me," Sunni demanded. Tuesday immediately followed orders, pulling her legs back with her hands.

The sight of Tuesday, naked, with her slick pussy open and ready for her was breathtaking. Her labia glistened with the evidence of her arousal, while her swollen clit waited for her attention.

Sunni reached over to a drawer in her desk, having hid a dildo in there a long time ago. There had been plenty of times in the past if she was working late and feeling a little horny, she'd handle her business in the privacy of her own office.

"Why am I not surprised?" Tuesday chuckled, as Sunni brandished the large dildo.

"I'm always prepared," she admitted. She slid the tip of the cock in between her mate's slick labia, coating it with her nectar. She watched with bated breath as the cock disappeared into her Tuesday's greedy pussy. She pushed it all the way in, eliciting a moan from Tuesday. Her eyes were locked on the sight of the cock coming out of her lover, coated with her juices. She thrust it in again, loving how Tuesday's body jerked from the invasion. "Now be quiet, mate. We wouldn't want to make anyone out there jealous."

She leaned over and latched onto her mate's clit while she pounded the thick cock into Tuesday.

Now they would play a different game.

Who could climax the quietest.

CHAPTER NINE

Tuesday was flying high. Her business was picking up and she'd hired a secretary named Ester. Ester was an older wolf, looking for a small job now that all of her children were out of the house. They had hit it off right away. She ran the office with an iron fist. Tuesday wouldn't expect anything less from a woman who raised six boys.

And the best thing? She was mating the woman of her dreams.

Her mother and brother would be coming in tomorrow for the mating ceremony. After the mating, they would join the pack run where they would be presented to the pack as a couple after they placed their claiming marks on each other.

"Any other questions for me?" she asked the gentleman sitting across from her. He was the owner of the local mechanic shop, having come in for a consult. Her entire day had been filled with appointments with business owners and locals needing tax advice.

"No, I think you've answered all my questions," Liam said with a smile as he stood. She stood and walked around her desk to shake his hand. Tuesday was glad that this meeting was finally over with. Not that she didn't like the man or didn't want to help him. It was that she had her mate on her mind and it was the end of the day.

She was ready to go home.

"Great. Have Ester set up your next appointment on your way out." She opened the door to her office.

"Thanks, Tuesday. It's so great to have a local accountant in Moon Valley," Liam admitted, his face lighting up with a smile.

"It's great to be here. I have certainly fallen in love with the town." She smiled as he waved and moved over to Ester.

"Any other appointments for the day?" she called out.

"No, Tuesday. Liam was your last one for the day," Ester replied.

"Go ahead and get out of here when you're done,"

she instructed. It was Friday, and there was no need to work late.

"Thanks, Tuesday. See you Monday," Ester replied as she scheduled Liam for his next appointment.

Tuesday closed the door to her office and did a little dance. Her business was truly growing. Her phones had been ringing constantly as more businesses and locals discovered that her office was here. If her business continued on the road it was going, she may have to hire an assistant to help her.

Anxious to get to Sunni, she scurried around her office and packed her bag. They would be staying at her house this weekend since she lived closer to where the pack met for the monthly runs.

After ensuring that everything was closed up and the computer was shut down, she hurried from her office, finding Ester long gone. She locked up the office and made her way to her car.

Traffic was light, allowing her to make it home in record time. She could see the light on in the house as she pulled into the driveway.

Knowing that her mate was waiting for her was the best feeling in the world.

She had given Sunni her own key since they had officially decided that they would live in Tuesday's home. Exiting her car, she rushed up the steps to the house and slid her key in the lock. She pushed the door open and gasped at the sight that greeted her.

She closed the door behind her and took in the rose petals littering the floor.

Sunni.

She dropped her messenger bag and keys on the table by the door, and followed the trail of flowers that led toward the stairs. She slowly made her way up to the second level of her home and smiled. The trail headed toward her bedroom.

She pushed the door open to the master bedroom and paused as tears flooded her eyes.

A very naked Sunni was down on one knee with a small velvet black box in her hand.

"What are you doing?" Tuesday gasped.

"Proposing to you the way you deserve," Sunni replied.

"Naked?"

"I said, how you deserved." Sunni wagged her eyebrows at Tuesday, causing laughter to bubble out of her lips.

Only Sunni would propose naked.

"Well, I do like coming home to flowers and my mate naked, waiting on me," she admitted, pushing off the doorjamb. Her feet carried her to Sunni, and she began stripping off her clothes, not wanting Sunni to be the only one naked in the room.

"So how about it, baby?" Sunni asked, suddenly serious. Tuesday stood before her as she looked down at her mate. Sunni opened the box, revealing a large solitary diamond ring. "Mate with me."

Tears clouded her vision as she jerked her head in a nod. "Yes! I'll mate with you a million times!"

She held out her hand as Sunni slipped the ring on her finger. Shifters didn't need to rely on fancy jewelry. The mating mark and the scent of a mate was all the shifters needed. But the ring was for their human side to show that she was taken.

"I love you," she murmured as Sunni stood. She couldn't wait for tomorrow where they would mark each other, and then be presented to the pack mates.

"I love you too, baby," Sunni assured, bringing her hand up to her lips so she could place a kiss on Tuesday's new ring.

She wrapped her arms around Sunni, bringing her close to her. Their breasts were crushed together as Tuesday leaned in and covered Sunni's mouth with hers.

Sunni took control of the kiss and kissed her within an inch of her life. She broke away, breathing hard, unable to catch her breath. Her body trembled from the heated gaze that Sunni gave her.

"I want you to make love to me," Tuesday whispered.

"Oh, I plan to." Tuesday knew that they would be spending the night at home. Sunni guided Tuesday over to the bed and laid her on her stomach. Sunni kneeled beside her, brushing her hair to the side to expose her full back. Tuesday shivered as Sunni blazed a hot trail of kisses along her back. "I love you, Tuesday Webb."

"I love you too, Sunni Vinson." Tuesday gasped. She was amazed at how her body responded to her mate's touch. Sunni ran her hand along the soft skin of Tuesday's back.

"I can't wait to make you mine," Sunni murmured.

"I'm already yours," Tuesday said as Sunni shifted on the bed. She parted Tuesday's ass cheeks wide as she trailed her tongue along, swirling it around Tuesday's puckered dark hole. A deep moan tore from Tuesday as she thrust her ass farther into Sunni's face, demanding more. She felt wanton, putting her ass in the air for her mate to do as she pleased. She buried her face into the pillow as she felt Sunni shift on the bed. The sounds of her nightstand opening peeked Tuesday's curiosity.

What was she pulling out of her drawer of toys?

She moved to turn so that she could see, but was rewarded with a firm slap to her ass cheek. Her body jerked in response, but she smiled, loving the dominating Sunni.

"No peeking," Sunni chuckled. Tuesday groaned, embracing the stinging sensation on her cheek. Moisture seeped from her pussy and she secretly wanted Sunni to do it again. She trusted her mate would take very good care of her. She waved her ass in the air, waiting to see what her mate was going to do to her.

She let loose a shriek as something slid along her slick folds, gathering some of her slickness. She rotated her hips, offering her pussy or ass to Sunni, whichever she wanted.

"Sunni," she groaned as the object slid in between her labia, before it slid toward her dark hole. Sunni used her fingers to gather moisture and spread it to her anus, preparing her. Her mate pushed something thick into her ass, eliciting a cry of ecstasy from Tuesday. Her body trembled from the fullness the plug gave her, stretching her dark hole. "Sunny, please."

"Don't worry, mate. I'm going to take care of you. Really good care of you," Sunny assured her as she slid a thick dildo deep within her core. She breathed through the sensations of both her holes being stretched wide. All of Sunni's dildos were thick cocks that had brought both of them much pleasure.

Tuesday cried out from the double penetration. Sunni began to pound the thick cock into her pussy, and Tuesday knew that she wasn't going to last long.

This orgasm was going to be hard and fast.

"Play with your clit, Tuesday."

Oh yes. Fast and hard.

Being the good little submissive wolf, she did as she was told.

A LETTER TO THE READER

Dear Reader,

Thank you for taking the time to read Moon Valley Shifters! I hope that you enjoyed reading these stories as much as I enjoyed writing them. Please feel free to leave a review to let me know your thoughts. I love reading reviews from my readers. Even if you didn't like it, I would love to know why. Reviews can be left on the platform you purchased the book, and even Goodreads!

Make sure you will explore one of the other books I have available!

Love,
Ariel Marie

ABOUT ARIEL MARIE

Ariel Marie is an author who loves the paranormal, action and hot steamy romance. She combines all three in each and every one of her stories. For as long as she can remember, she has loved vampires, shifters and every creature you can think of. This even rolls over into her favorite movies. She loves a good action packed thriller! Throw a touch of the supernatural world in it and she's hooked!

Sign up for Ariel Marie's Newsletter

Ariel puts this together to give her readers updates! Her subscribers are usually one of the first to learn about her releases, ARC signups and giveaways!

Newsletter

ALSO BY ARIEL MARIE

An Erotic Vampire Series

Vampire Destiny

Moon Valley Shifters Box Set (F/F Shifters)

Lyric's Mate

Meadow's Mate

Tuesday's Mate

The Dark Shadows Series

Princess

Toma

Phaelyn

Teague

Adrian

Nicu

The Mirrored Prophecy Series

Power of the Fae

Fight for the Fae

Future of the Fae (TBD)

The Dragon Curse Series (Ménage MFF Erotic Series)

Mating Two Dragons

Loving Two Dragons

Claiming Two Dragons

Taking Two Dragons

Sassy Ever After Kindle World

Her Warrior Dragon

Her Fierce Dragon

Her Guardian Dragon (TBD)

Stand Alone Book

Dani's Return

A Faery's Kiss

Fourteen Shades of F*cked Up: An Anthology

Tiger Haven

Searching For His Mate

12 Magical Nights of Christmas Anthology

A Tiger's Gift

Sin & Seduction Box Set

Dark Rising: A Paranormal and Fantasy Romance Limited Edition Collection